FROGSPELL

C. J. Busby

templar

To Zoe, Max and Izzy

A TEMPLAR BOOK

First published in the UK in 2011 by Templar Publishing,
an imprint of The Templar Company Limited,
The Granary, North Street, Dorking, Surrey, RH4 1DN, UK
www.templarco.co.uk

First UK edition

3 5 7 9 10 8 6 4

ISBN 978-1-84877-139-0

MIX
Paper from
responsible sources
FSC® C020852

Printed and bound by CPI Group
(UK) Ltd, Croydon, CR0 4YY

Frogspell

Contents

An Accidental Spell

The day that Max accidentally discovered the frogspell started like any ordinary day in Castle Perilous. He and his sister, Olivia, were having breakfast late, as usual. Olivia had been trying to teach her pet dragon, Adolphus, a new trick, and Max had been making plans for his new spell. He was still studying his spell book at the dining table while absent-mindedly chewing a sausage, and Olivia was happily enjoying her second bowl of porridge.

Suddenly their mum, Lady Griselda Pendragon, burst into the dining hall, in a hurry as usual, and tripped over Adolphus.

"Aaarrrghhh!! Drat that dragon! Max! I need my broomstick! Have you been using it again? You know what Dad said last time."

Max looked up from his breakfast. He couldn't actually remember what Dad had said last time, but he could make a pretty good guess. Sir Bertram Pendragon was a gruff, burly knight with a large moustache and a deep voice. He liked nothing better than a good flagon of ale and a trusty enemy to whack with his big sword, and he wasn't fond of wizardry. He considered it cheating. He tolerated Lady Griselda's witchiness and allowed Max to learn a few spells and potions, but he did not at all approve of letting Max ride a broomstick. It was too girly.

Max sighed. His father had probably threatened to make him sleep in the pigsty if he were ever caught on it again.

"Max!" said his mother again, loudly. "Did you leave it somewhere?"

Max considered. He'd certainly used the broomstick recently, because he remembered pushing Olivia into the moat with it when they were pretending to be Sir Gawaine and the Black Knight of Doom.

He glanced over at his sister. She was wearing a long green dress and looking demure, but it was misleading. She spent most of her time wrestling with the squires or mucking about in the stables. It was a miracle he'd actually managed to push her in the moat – usually it was the other way round. Max was slight for his eleven years, with light brown hair that fell untidily around his freckled face. And he was not particularly well coordinated, so he usually missed any target he was trying to hit.

Suddenly he remembered where the broomstick was. He'd taken it to fly up to the top of the Bell Tower to rescue Adolphus, who had somehow got himself stuck after chasing the castle cat up there. Then Adolphus had been too scared to sit on the back of the broom so he'd had to carry him all the way back down the winding staircase.

"I think you'll find the broom is at the top of the Bell Tower, Mum," said Max, returning to his toast. "I saw Olivia take it up there when she was playing with her dolls."

Olivia looked up from her porridge and opened her mouth to protest that this was absolutely not true – she didn't even possess a doll – and Max was a slimeball... But Mum had gone and all that was left in the kitchen was a trail of green smoke.

"You are a big fat liar, Max," said Olivia, flicking a spoonful of porridge at him. He ducked, and kicked her hard under the table.

"Oww! I'll get you for that!"

"Just try," said Max, getting off his chair and heading for the door. "But it'll have to be later, because I'm busy this morning. Leave me alone or I'll turn your face purple with my new spell."

And with that he headed off to the Spell Room, to practise it.

The Spell Room was in the cellar of the castle, down a steep stone stairway with cobwebs swinging gently from the ceiling. Max loved it down there. It was where he got to experiment with cooking up his own spells and potions, and generally where he escaped to avoid sword practice with his father. Last week Sir Bertram had accidentally whacked off a squire's fingers while demonstrating a particularly tricky manoeuvre, and although Lady Griselda had managed to magic the fingers back on, Max didn't fancy being the next victim. He had a better plan.

In under a week, the Annual Festival of Magic would take place at Castle Camelot, and Max was determined to have perfected a really spectacular bit of magic for the Novices' Spell-Making Competition. Apart from the prize money of twenty gold coins, winning this might finally prove to Dad that Max was a natural wizard who should forget about knight school and concentrate on spells. So far, Sir Bertram had resisted all Max's pleas, insisting that he just needed to try harder and he'd make a very decent knight. But Max didn't like horses at all, and the last time he had tried to skewer the practice dummy with a lance he had almost skewered Sir Bertram instead, who was standing twenty yards away.

In general, Max was a lot better at spells than he was at horse riding or swordplay. But the annual Novices' Competition had not been a lucky one for him so far, mainly due to Adrian Hogsbottom, Max's worst enemy. He couldn't remember when Snotty Hogsbottom had first proved himself to be the kingdom's slimiest toadwart, but it was a long time since either of them had had a civil word for the other. The year before last, Snotty had caused the stage to burst into flames just as Max's carefully controlled firework spell was coming to a triumphant conclusion. Max had been blamed, and Snotty had won. And Max's freckled face turned pink just thinking about last year's competition.

He'd tried to magic a bucket to carry water from the castle well but it had simply turned itself upside down and crash-landed on the examiner's head. Snotty had won again. This year he really had to get it right.

As Max dabbled and mixed and consulted his spell books, a voice floated down the stairwell.

"Max! I'm off to cook up a spell at Castle Pendennis – Lady Alys wants a beauty potion for the ball tonight... Dad's at the Round Table meeting but Mrs Mudfoot will keep an eye on you."

"Yeah, okay," called back Max, concentrating as he added a scattering of silver dragonfly wings to the cauldron and watched blue steam rise up to the ceiling. Mrs Mudfoot was the castle cook. She had twenty chins and twice as many hairy warts, and was always looking for an excuse to put Max in one of her cooking pots and make him into a tasty stew. He made a mental note to keep well out of her way.

"Be good – look after Olivia! And don't cause any trouble!"

"Yes, yes, fine!" called Max impatiently, waiting for the right moment to add the slivers of river's root.

As Mum left, he turned back to the mixture in the cauldron, which was starting to smell like dirty feet. Perfect! As he added the slivers one by one, he didn't notice Olivia creeping down the stone stairs to lurk in the darkest corner of the cellar.

When the last sliver of river's root had been added, the mixture turned purple and started to smell like buttery crumpets.

"Yes!" Max punched the air, then looked at the spell book again. "Now it's just the snails' toenails." He looked round the room for the jar and spotted a shadow in the corner by the shelves. It looked suspiciously like Olivia. Max moved a bit closer. It was Olivia.

"Olivia! What are you doing here?! I told you to leave me alone this morning! You're asking to be spelled!"

"Yeah, right," said Olivia, unimpressed.

"Like last time, when you tried to make my nose grow longer and all that happened was I sneezed twice. Big scare, Max."

Max narrowed his eyes. "For your information, Snotface, I didn't try to make your nose grow longer, I just said I was going to, so you'd go away. But this time I really will turn you purple if you don't leave me in peace."

"Well, I don't think that would be a very good idea seeing as Mum said you had to look after me. And besides, I thought you said something about needing snails' toenails to finish the spell?" Olivia held up a dark-blue glass jar that she'd been concealing behind her dress and looked smug.

"Olivia! Give me that!" said Max crossly. Honestly! Olivia was such a pest! All he wanted was a little peace and quiet to finally get this spell right for the competition. It wasn't much to ask, surely?

Olivia considered this, looking at the jar in her hands.

"I'll give it to you, Max, if you promise to

come and show me that disarming manoeuvre Dad taught you yesterday," she said.

Max groaned. Sword practice with Olivia was always a painful affair. If he wasn't skewering his own foot, she was doing it for him. Neither of them was very good – Olivia because she wasn't actually allowed to use a sword at all, Max because he was just naturally talentless. But Olivia insisted on getting all the practice she could and she was getting relentlessly better.

"Okay," he sighed. "Now hand over the jar, quick."

He strode across the room to get the jar of snails' toenails. But as he reached out for it, Olivia spotted his pet rat, Ferocious, poking his head out from the top of Max's tunic.

"Max! You're not allowed to have Ferocious down here! Mum told you!" she said accusingly. "He's disgusting anyway, he's probably got fleas..."

Ferocious, offended, jumped out at Olivia, who fended him off with one hand but missed, and whacked Max instead. Max overbalanced and, throwing out his arms as he fell, swept a tall green jar off the nearby shelf. There was an awful crash, as the jar shattered, and little bouncy balls of bat's-squeak-breath flew across the room.

Max, sprawled on the floor, watched in horror as three blue balls bounced right into the cauldron and sank into the purple liquid. There was a moment's pause, and then...

BANG!

The contents of the cauldron exploded and dollops of sticky, blue gunk flew around the cellar. One landed on Max, one landed on Olivia and one landed on Ferocious. They barely had time to blink when the room went all shivery and strange and seemed to grow rather larger.

Olivia was now a purple frog with red spots. Ferocious was a red frog with purple spots. And Max was an extremely angry-looking orange frog with bright blue spots.

A Vital Ingredient

There was a shocked silence as the frogs stared at each other.

"Well that was quite spectacular, wasn't it?" said Ferocious grumpily. "You two never stop arguing! No wonder things go wrong. And now here I am, horrid and small and slimy – and worst of all – with no tail!"

"Ferocious – you can talk!" spluttered Max.

"Of course I can talk!" said Ferocious with scorn. "I always could. It's just you couldn't understand me before, because you're not a rat. And nor am I, any more, thanks to you," he added, stretching out one webbed foot and looking at it gloomily.

"Well," said Olivia, recovering rapidly from the shock of being small, fat and purple. "You seem to have actually done a spell, Max. Blow me down with a puff of bat's-squeak-breath. Now what are you going to do?"

Max put his head on one side and considered.

"Well... personally, I think you look much better as a frog, Olivia, so I'm not sure I'll be doing anything. And besides, it's your fault the wrong stuff got in the spell, so maybe it's you that should be doing something."

Olivia narrowed her eyes and was about to give Max a piece of her mind, when a small fly buzzed past. In a blink, her tongue whipped out and pulled the fly in and her mouth shut on it like a trap.

She chewed thoughtfully.

"Wow, I can't believe you just did that!" said Max, awed.

"Mmm," Olivia licked her lips. "Neither can I. But it was delicious. Like a flying strawberry ice cream."

Max looked round to see if he could spot another. Once you started to look, with super-enhanced, fly-spotting frog-vision, you could see they were everywhere. Soon Max and Olivia were snapping up flies like experts and discussing whether they tasted more of strawberry ice cream or blueberry crumble.

"Erhem! When you two have quite finished..." said Ferocious after a few minutes. "Maybe we could get back to the issue of HOW WE GET CHANGED BACK! I don't want to spend the rest of my life as a frog. I liked being a rat."

Max regretfully let a particularly juicy-looking fly escape and turned to Ferocious.

"I don't know. I suppose I could look in my

spell book – but as far as I know, no one has ever found a spell to turn people into frogs before, so there's not likely to be a spell to turn them back."

"I thought people got turned into frogs all the time?" said Olivia, surprised.

"No, that's just in fairy stories," said Max scornfully.

"Oh, great," said Ferocious. "I'm a frog, and it's not even a spell anyone knows anything about because it's never been done before. Great."

But Max was not listening. He was standing completely still, running over what he'd just said in his head. No one's ever found a spell to turn people into frogs before. No one's ever...

"That's it!" he spluttered.

"A reversal spell?" said Olivia hopefully.

"No, idiot! I've invented a new spell! No one's ever done it before! I'm going to win the Novices' Spell-Making Competition! I'm going to beat Snotty Hogsbottom!! And Dad will have to let me train to be a wizard and stop all this stupid knight nonsense! I'm made! I'll be famous!"

"Except no one will know it's you who's won and you won't be allowed to enter anyway, because in case you hadn't noticed, you're now a frog," Ferocious pointed out.

Max came back to earth with a squelch. Ferocious was right. He couldn't enter the Novices' Competition as a frog. And he could only imagine what Mum and Dad would say if they returned to find their children gone without a trace and three multicoloured frogs in their place. How could he change them back? He needed a plan.

"I suppose we could look in the spell book," he said at last. "There might be some kind of general reversal spell."

The three frogs hopped across the flagstones to where the spell book lay open on the floor. Turning the stiff, yellowed pages with webbed feet was not the easiest task. Reading the words was even more difficult. Frog-vision might be fabulous for picking out flies in a dark cellar, but words just looked like blurry squiggles.

"I think this one says something about a reversal spell," said Olivia, sticking her tongue out in concentration.

"Don't ask me," said Ferocious. "I couldn't read as a rat and definitely can't as a frog. It's down to you two."

Max pored over the spell. Olivia was right, there was something there.

"A General Reversal Spell for Most Charms and Hexes," he read slowly. "That might do it! What are the ingredients?"

"Cobweb fronds, rose-tinted sunset powder, ground hedgehog spines and – er – black... peppercorns," said Olivia, squinting.

"Black peppercorns?!" said Max in horror. "But they're kept in the kitchen!"

Olivia's round frog's eyes looked at him sympathetically.

"Oh dear, Max. In the kitchen. But seeing as you're the one that got us into this mess, I guess that means..."

"Nooooo!" howled Max. "I can't! I'll have to get past Mrs Mudfoot, and she's bound to put me in a stew or squish me into frog jam or worse..."

"Tough," said Ferocious decisively. "You need to be a boy, I want to be a rat, and fetching as your sister looks in purple with red spots, your parents won't be best pleased if she stays that way. Face it, Max, it's for the greater good."

***

Max crept along the corridor leading to the kitchen, staying as close as he could to the damp grey stone walls and hoping the shadows made his bright orange colouring a little less noticeable. The heavy oak door to the kitchen was half open and behind it he could hear Mrs Mudfoot muttering to herself.

"Namby pamby vegetable soup, huh... Need some nice cows' brains in there, give it a bit of flavour..."

Max poked his head round the door. He could see a large bottom poking up in the air as the cook bent over to pick up bunches of muddy carrots from the basket at her feet. Her long grey skirts hung in grimy folds and he could see her meaty hands grabbing two bunches from the pile. He really didn't want to get anywhere near those hands...

"Wash 'em, she says, when the mud's the only bit with any taste. Fussy beggars, bit of mud never hurt anyone..."

She turned to the sink and dipped the carrots in some water for the blink of an eye, then dumped them on the long wooden table and began to chop them with a huge meat cleaver. Chop! Chop! Chop!

With each chop, Max flinched. He crept round the door and tiptoed (as much as he could with webbed feet) into the shadow of the big spice cupboard. This was where the pepper would be. Nearly there now. All well so far.

He swallowed. Who was he kidding? The most difficult part was still to come.

Checking that Mrs Mudfoot was still occupied with the carrots, Max glanced up at the spice cupboard. Which drawer would have peppercorns? He hopped closer and looked at the label on the nearest drawer. 'Mustard Seed' it said, in neat black writing. It was at the bottom of the cupboard, near the floor. Just above was 'Saffron', and across from that was 'Frog's Legs'. Max shuddered. And then he spotted it. The pepper drawer... Right at the top of the cupboard, in full sight of Mrs Mudfoot's gleaming black eyes...

Max nearly gave up there and then. He really couldn't see any way he was going to get to that drawer, let alone get it open, get the peppercorns out and escape from the kitchen without being squished into a frog pancake or put in the soup to give it some flavour. He sighed. Maybe he would be better off just heading for the castle pond and making friends with the other frogs. He could spend the rest of his life happily jumping from lily pad to lily pad and eating apple-crumble-flavoured insects. But the thought of Snotty Hogsbottom winning the Spell-Making trophy for the third year running was too much to bear. Max had to get those peppercorns.

Mrs Mudfoot finished chopping the carrots and turned towards the cupboard. Max froze.

"Right then. Nasty herbs now, fresh from the garden. At least there'll be some nice bugs on 'em to spice it up, eh?" She turned heavily and stomped off towards the door, carrying the basket. Max nearly did a triple somersault on the spot. Brilliant! he thought. She's going to get herbs from the garden! I'll be alone in the kitchen!

He hopped onto a nearby stool and carefully measured the leap to the top of the spice cupboard. It seemed miles away – but then he was a frog. He flexed his powerful back legs and jumped.

He hit the edge of the cupboard with a thump! that knocked the wind out of him, grabbed the top with his front legs, and scrabbled furiously with his back feet. After what seemed like a week of hanging dangerously on the edge, Max managed to haul himself up over the top. Phew! He looked down over the edge at the drawers. There it was –

'Peppercorns' – with a shiny brass handle to pull the drawer out.

Max sat back on his haunches and pondered. Being a frog rather than a boy, and being on the top of the cupboard rather than in front of it, made opening the drawer just a bit trickier. At last, he decided that the best way would be to lie on his stomach and push it open with his back legs.

Max stretched out flat and hooked his back feet into the brass handle of the drawer. Then he took a deep breath and pushed. The drawer went flying open, and he slid helplessly after it, across the shiny surface of the cupboard, until he was just clinging on to the edge with all his strength.

Just then he heard the door open and Mrs Mudfoot come into the room. Max looked up – his front feet slipped – and he plunged face first into the darkness of the peppercorn drawer.

Dragon to the Rescue

Adolphus the pet dragon was sniffing around the castle entrance looking for woodlice quite unaware of the danger Max and Olivia were in. There were usually woodlice to be found crawling about behind the big wooden door, in the damp, dark of the hallway, and Adolphus found them fascinating. When he got bored with watching them scurrying around, he found them pretty tasty too.

Adolphus twisted his scaly, blue-green body right round into the darkest corner and waved his forked tail happily as he spotted several woodlice beetling across the corridor. Just as he was about to breathe a little fire to encourage them to run around more, he heard a peculiar noise and looked up.

There was something small and red at the other end of the corridor. Actually, there were two small things, one red and one purple – and they smelled very strongly of pondweed. Adolphus took flight and glided down the hall to investigate.

He landed in a tangled heap of wings and legs in front of two strangely coloured frogs who looked up at him in horror. Adolphus sniffed the red one. Maybe it would taste nice? But before he could open his mouth, the other frog shouted at him.

"Adolphus! Stop it this minute! Bad dragon! You are not to eat that frog!"

Adolphus stopped. He felt a bit confused.

The voice was coming from the purple frog – but it sounded like the voice of his mistress, Olivia Pendragon. He looked down at it.

"Um, please? Are you Olivia?"

"Yes, yes, I am!" said the purple frog. Olivia was incredibly relieved. She'd thought Ferocious was dragon-dinner for sure – but it seemed Adolphus could understand frogs and had even recognised her. This was nothing short of miraculous because Adolphus was not the brainiest of young dragons and generally ate first and asked questions later.

"Adolphus," she said. "We've been turned into frogs by one of Max's stupid spells. And now he's gone to get peppercorns from the kitchen and he's been gone ages and we're afraid Mrs Mudfoot's put him in the soup."

"She's almost definitely put him in the soup," added Ferocious. "Probably us next if we carry on standing here."

"Oh no! Oh dear! Max in the soup! What can I do to help?" said Adolphus anxiously, flapping his wings and hopping from foot to foot.

"Try not to squash us, for a start," pointed out Ferocious, jumping smartly out of the way of Adolphus's claws.

"We're on our way to the kitchen," said Olivia. "Max is in there somewhere and he probably needs rescuing. Come on!"

The three of them set off across the corridor and crept down the passageway to the kitchen. At the door, they stopped and peered carefully round. Mrs Mudfoot was stirring the large cauldron on the stove and gradually adding handfuls of something suspiciously grey and smelly. Olivia looked around the room carefully, then turned to the others.

"There's an open drawer at the top of the spice cupboard. I bet it's the pepper drawer. Max must have got up there and opened it. But I can't see him anywhere."

Ferocious hopped across to the cupboard and looked up at the drawer. Then he looked around on the floor and spotted a stray hazelnut that had rolled under a nearby stool. He picked it up, measured the distance carefully, and chucked the nut up at the drawer. It hit the front with a sharp thud.

They froze, but Mrs Mudfoot didn't appear to have heard. A few minutes later, they saw the tips of two orange feet appear over the edge of the drawer and a voice floated down to them.

"Olivia! Ferocious! I'm stuck! It's too deep to clamber out and I've tried jumping out but there's not enough space – I just keep banging my head on the top. Do something, quick – before Mrs Mudfoot finds me and puts me in a pie!"

Olivia and the others retreated behind the door to consider the situation.

"This is an emergency," said Olivia. "We've got to get him out before she finds him."

"And we've got to get the peppercorns or we're frogs forever," added Ferocious. "In fact, I'd say that was the first priority, myself, much as I love dear old Max."

"You'll have to do it, Adolphus," said Olivia

decisively. "You need to fly up to the drawer, get Max in your claws and fly him back down to the cauldron in the cellar."

"Peppercorns," corrected Ferocious. "Get peppercorns in your claws. Max too, if you can, but no good having Max back unless we've got the all-important spell ingredients."

"Both of them," said Olivia. "Peppercorns and Max – to the cellar for the spell. Got that, Adolphus?"

"Right. Yes. Okay," said Adolphus eagerly. "Fly up to the drawer, eat the peppercorns and then put Max in the cauldron."

"No!" said Olivia. "Concentrate, Adolphus! Max from the drawer to the cellar and the peppercorns from the drawer to the cauldron."

"Oh, right!" said Adolphus apologetically. "So, it's Max to go into the peppercorns and the drawer to go to the cellar."

"Adolphus!" groaned Olivia. "Max – and – the – peppercorns – to – the – cellar!"

"This is going to be a disaster," said Ferocious, covering his face with his webbed feet.

***

Adolphus skittered round the kitchen door, and looked quickly round the room to see where Mrs Mudfoot was. She seemed to be busy stirring something suspiciously brown and sticky into the soup. Adolphus flew up to the top of the cupboard with a few wingbeats and peered down into the peppercorn drawer. There was a bright orange frog sitting at the bottom, along with several packets of pepper.

Adolphus considered the situation. Pepper – he needed pepper, that's what Olivia had said. And there was something about Max. But there was no Max in the drawer – just a strange orange frog. Adolphus scratched behind his ear and pondered. Perhaps Max wanted Adolphus to bring him the pepper? That must be it. But where was Max? Oh, yes! He remembered now! Max was in the cellar.

Adolphus picked up a packet of pepper in one

claw, then considered the frog. You never know, it might be tasty. But he had to take the pepper to Max. Perhaps he could bring the frog along too and eat it later? Carefully he picked up the frog in his mouth, ignoring its croaks, and prepared to fly out of the kitchen.

But Mrs Mudfoot had finished with the soup and was heading over to get her morning snack of pickled snail's-foot fancy from the spice cupboard.

"Oh no!" gasped Olivia from the doorway. "I can't look!"

Ferocious lifted one webbed foot from in front of his face. "We're doomed," he said. "Doomed."

Mrs Mudfoot took one look at Adolphus perched on top of the cupboard and before you could say 'snail's-foot fancy' she had him by the scruff of the neck with her meaty hands.

"Got you, you pestiferous little runty worm's spawn," she growled. "In my kitchen! Stealing my peppercorns! And what's that you've got in your good-for-nothing mouth?"

Eeek, thought Adolphus. Caught by the terrible Mudfoot. He was never going to get those peppercorns to Max now. Best distract her with the frog.

Adolphus shook his head to and fro, waving the frog around in front of Mrs Mudfoot's face. The frog squealed and wriggled its back legs desperately.

"You foul beast!" shouted Mrs Mudfoot, and squeezed harder. Adolphus spat the frog out onto the floor, where it lay twitching feebly, and breathed fire at the cook, who let go of him, cursing horribly. While she frantically blew on her scorched fingers, he flew across and out of the kitchen in a flash of blue-green scales.

Mrs Mudfoot bent down over the twitching orange frog.

"Well, well, my beauty. What did the nasty horrible dragon do to you, then?"

Max opened one eye. The huge red face of the cook was bearing down on him, glistening with sweat, her many chins wobbling as she spoke . She scooped him up in her large hands and lifted him even closer. Max could see the long black hairs coming out of each of her huge warts. He shuddered.

"What a sweetie-pie you are, then," crooned the cook. "What a little darling froggy. Did the horrid dragon hurt you? Let Mummy give you a big kiss better, how about that?"

Max opened his frog's eyes wide in horror. What?! She was going to kiss him?! Mrs Mudfoot?!

"No, no, please, no..." he whimpered, but there was no way out of it. The cook's jowly chins were wobbling towards him, her warts bobbing up and down, her lips puckered...

"Aaaaarrrggghhh!!" shrieked Max.

"Aaaaarrrggghhh!!" shrieked Mrs Mudfoot.

Max suddenly found himself on the floor in a sprawl of limbs and Mrs Mudfoot had her hands up in the air and was backing away towards the table. The moment that her lips had touched the slimy orange frog, it had exploded in a shower of sparks and in its place was...

That dratted boy, Max Pendragon! Mrs Mudfoot gritted her teeth and stopped backing away. In one smooth movement, she whipped a large meat cleaver off the table and advanced.

Max scrambled to his feet and ran for his life. As he dashed through the open door, it slammed shut behind him and the bolt was rammed home. He turned to see Adolphus with his shoulder against the door and two frogs pushing on the bolt.

"Quick!" said the purple one. "Pick us up and make for the cellar!"

Max grabbed the frogs and pelted down the corridor. He flailed round the corner and tumbled down the cellar steps, turning back to slam the door behind them. They could hear footsteps following them down, Mrs Mudfoot's large, heavy feet slapping on the stone floor. Max fumbled in his belt pouch frantically – ah! he had it! He pulled out the large iron key and locked the heavy cellar door. He slid down the last few steps and collapsed onto a pile of tapestries lying at the bottom. Mrs Mudfoot gave the cellar door a few token smacks with her fist, but it was six inches thick and strengthened with iron bands. She knew when she was defeated. Max heard her heavy tread going back up the steps, and only then did he dare to take breath.

"Well," said Ferocious, after they had recovered slightly. "That was a narrow escape. But at least now we know how to reverse the spell. Much as it pains me to say it, I think a bit of kissing is called for, Max."

"Excuse me," said Max, still shuddering from the memory of being kissed by Mrs Mudfoot. "I think I might need a bit of recovery time, a large bribe and a large amount of begging before I can even think about kissing two slimy frogs."

"Hey, Max!" said Olivia. "You can still understand us!"

"So I can," said Max, interested. "It must be an after-effect of having been turned into an animal. I wonder. However – back to the subject of bribery..."

Ferocious hopped onto Max's shoulder and hissed into his ear.

"Max! Kiss me back into being a rat right now or I will stick my long slimy frog's tongue deep into your ear and poke your brains out through your nostrils."

"Mmm, well – when you put it like that," said Max hurriedly, and kissed Ferocious on the nose.

Whoosh!

In a shower of sparks, he was a long-tailed black rat once more, sitting on Max's shoulder and calmly cleaning his whiskers.

"Thanks," he said. "Much obliged, I'm sure."

"Wow!" said Adolphus. "That was amazing! Do it again, Max! Please! I want to see Olivia go whoosh! Up in stars!"

Max looked at Olivia. She looked back with solemn frog's eyes.

"I suppose it has to be done," said Max.

"I guess I have to put up with it," said Olivia. Max took a deep breath and bent down to kiss the top of her froggy head. Olivia shut her eyes.

Whoosh!

She was surrounded by a haze of sparkly stars and was definitely a girl – with long dark plaits and a cheerful face, and not a touch of purple anywhere. Adolphus whooped and flew around the room.

"Well that's that, then," said Ferocious, satisfied as he burrowed down into Max's tunic to go to sleep.

Max looked at Olivia and grinned with relief. They were safe from the awful Mudfoot. They were themselves again. And he had a great spell to kick Snotty Hogsbottom's bottom with in three days' time.

"You know," he said, happily. "I'll need an assistant for the Novices' Spell-Making Competition. To demonstrate the incredible power of my never-seen-before spell. And of course, whoever did it would certainly get a share of the twenty gold coins prize money... to say nothing of the eternal glory!"

Olivia grinned. "Yeah, yeah, OK," she said. "I'll be turned into a frog for you. I'll even share the prize money fifty-fifty. I hate Snotty Hogsbottom, too. He trod on my toes three times at the Trophy Ball last year and he called Adolphus a pea-brain."

"Adolphus is a pea-brain," said Ferocious, poking his head briefly out of Max's tunic and then settling back down to sleep.

"That's beside the point," said Olivia, firmly. "Snotty Hogsbottom is a stuck-up pig and needs to be taught a lesson. Besides, if Dad has to give up on you becoming a knight, maybe he'll let me be a squire, instead. I'm in!"

"Right, then," said Max. "We'll need to brew up some of that reversal spell. No good just kissing you back – that makes it look far too easy. I want it all to look as impressive and magical as possible. There's no way I'm letting Snotty Hogsbottom beat me this time!"

Hogsbottom's Secret

astle Camelot was decorated from moat to turrets in silver streamers and multicoloured balloons. The sun was shining, and there was music floating across the castle green from the many minstrels and jesters hoping to please the crowds with tales of brave knights and their daring deeds. Brightly coloured stalls flourished round the edges of the green, selling an amazing variety of trinkets:

jester hats, cauldrons, jars of potions, decorated scabbards, fried rats' tails and toy broomsticks. There was a crowd of assorted knights and ladies weaving in and out of the stalls and children, dragons, dogs and other small animals were diving around in their midst getting in everyone's way. Above the castle entrance, a large banner proclaimed: Annual Festival of Magic.

"Mmm, roast suckling pig," said Max, sniffing the air appreciatively as smells of cooking food wafted across from numerous campfires. He, Olivia and their parents were approaching the castle entrance slowly, fighting their way through the crowds, with Adolphus held tightly on a strong lead. They had rooms in the castle itself, since Sir Bertram was a distant cousin of King Arthur, but Max was slightly envious of the families camped around the castle in their bright tents, enjoying the sunshine.

When they got to the entrance, they were stopped by two rather surly-looking guards.

"Pass, please," said one of them in a bored voice, holding his hand out.

"Pass?" roared Sir Bertram. "Pass?! Don't you know who I am, you good-for-nothing scurvy sons of kitchen wenches? What do you mean, pass?"

The guard looked up and squinted.

"Oh – er – yes, good day, Sir Bertram," he said, nervously. "Orders, I'm afraid. All visitors to show passes, no exceptions whatsoever. It's on account of having the young princeling here, you know – the son of the Cornish King." He lowered his voice a fraction and added, "They do say as how there's a plot to do away with him while he's here, and of course that'll mean war – the Cornish are looking for any excuse to invade as it is, and if anything happens to the young prince while he's under the king's protection, well, that's all the excuse they'll need..."

"So if you don't mind," said the other guard, holding out his hand in turn. "Pass, please." He took a step backwards as Sir Bertram swelled visibly, but before his face had time to turn the colour of a ripe tomato (which Max knew was the danger point), Lady Griselda had whipped out a piece of creamy parchment from her robes and handed it over.

"I think you'll find this is what you need," she said sweetly. "Don't fuss, Bertram," she added, turning to her husband. "You know they need to be extra careful."

"Absolute nonsense," muttered Sir Bertram. "Dashed insult, that's what I call it. Balderdash and poppycock!" But he consented to let the guards examine the pass before sweeping them all into the castle and up to their rooms at the top of the north tower.

Lady Griselda started bustling about, unpacking cauldrons and spell ingredients and her best robes, and Sir Bertram stomped off to find some friends to join him in a practice round for the 'Knight Who Can Quaff the Most Ale in a Single Swallow' competition, which he generally won. Max winked at Olivia, and they set to work helping to unpack in the most unhelpful way possible, with the biggest number of annoying questions they could think of. Meanwhile, Adolphus flew around the room getting periodically tangled up in the tapestries. After five minutes, Lady Griselda had had enough.

"Oh, for goodness' sake, go and practise your spells or something and leave me in peace! I'll be quicker by myself! And take that dratted dragon with you."

"Thanks, Mum," said Max, happily dumping the pile of clothes he was holding, and they set off down the turret staircase with Adolphus skittering down the stone steps behind them.

They headed straight for the west wing, where they knew there were always empty rooms. Merlin lived in this part of the castle, and most people were keen to avoid any confrontation with the extremely powerful wizard. Max, however, thought everything he'd heard about Merlin was brilliant, and was always hoping they would run into the wizard so he could finally meet him and tell him so – but so far they never had.

"Right," said Max, as they settled into a small room with narrow windows, off the fourth-floor corridor. It was empty except for some old tapestries on the walls and a few bits of wooden furniture. "Time to practise the frogspell antidote and check the reversal works."

They had brewed up the general reversal spell the day before, as well as some carefully controlled frogspell potion, but they had not had time to test them before leaving for Camelot. The Novices' Spell-Making Competition was the next day, right at the end of the festival, so they had a day and a half to perfect their act.

"So," said Max, pulling one of his hunting gloves on to his right hand, "If you'll just stand there in the middle of the room..."

"I'm sorry?" said Olivia, pretending great surprise. "You were intending to try this out on me?"

"Yes, on you," said Max, slowly and deliberately.

"Seeing as you're my assistant, and seeing as assistants test potions, not wizards."

"Well," said Olivia, folding her arms and looking very determined. "Since you're not exactly a wizard, Max, and seeing as I'm doing you a very great favour by agreeing to be your assistant tomorrow, I think it's probably down to you to test your own potion today. I'm not getting turned into a pink elephant with green spots because you got one of the ingredients wrong, thank you!"

Max sighed. That was the trouble with younger sisters. They'd be fine for a while, almost like they were completely trustworthy, and then they'd let you down when you really needed them. Drat. He would just have to take the smelly potion himself, then.

"All right," he said, taking off his glove and handing it to her along with a translucent green glass bottle on a chain. "Here's the antidote to change me back and a glove to wear when you hold the frogspell potion. We wouldn't want you to accidentally get changed into a frog, now, would we?"

He carefully took a small blue bottle out of his belt pouch and shook Ferocious out at the same time.

"Oh, don't tell me," said Ferocious as he tumbled onto the stone floor. "You're about to voluntarily spell yourself into a frog. As if you didn't cause enough trouble the last time. Some people never learn."

"You know – sometimes I miss the days when I couldn't understand you, Ferocious," said Max, sighing. "This is important. It's going to get me out of sword practice for good and maybe save me from getting my arm chopped off in one of Dad's madder moments. Besides making Snotty Hogsbottom eat dirt."

"And it'll be fun!" added Adolphus excitedly. "Max will go whoosh! In stars!"

"Oh, right. Well, wake me up when the antidote doesn't work and I'll consider giving you a big wet rat kiss." And with that Ferocious curled up behind one of the trailing tapestries and went to sleep.

"Right," said Max, and took a deep breath. "Put my glove on and hold out your hand." He shook one little drop of blue gunk out of the bottle onto Olivia's gloved hand and then stowed the bottle in his pouch.

Olivia threw the blue gunk at Max's head.

BANG!

He disappeared, and in his place was a small orange frog with blue spots.

"Uurrghh!" he said. "I'd forgotten how weird it is, being changed into a frog."

"OK," said Olivia. "That worked. Now for the antidote."

She took the stopper out of the green bottle and prepared to shake a few drops onto the frog. But at that moment, the door to the room opened, and a loud, sneering voice interrupted them.

"Well, if it isn't little Olivia Pendragon in here all by herself. How nice to see you again. And where's your good-for-nothing brother?"

The boy in the doorway was tall and pale, with spiky, black hair and an expression of contempt. Behind him was a shorter, stockier boy with red hair and a pug face. His eyes were slightly squinting and he looked mean.

"Oh... hello, Sn–... er... Adrian," said Olivia nervously, putting the stopper back in the green bottle and throwing it hurriedly round her neck. "What are you doing here?"

She shuffled across in front of the frog, hoping Max would get a chance to hop under her skirt, but the movement caught Snotty Hogsbottom's attention and he dived for the floor.

"Aha!" he said, coming up with the orange frog held firmly between finger and thumb. "What a delightful creature! Your pet, Olivia?"

"Um, yes," said Olivia. "Give him back please! I need to – er – get back to our rooms to help Mother."

"Oh, I expect you do," drawled Snotty in a

bored voice. "But you see, I have some questions for you. And I don't feel like letting you have your frog back unless you answer them. Isn't that right, Jerome?"

The shorter boy nodded, and moved closer. Olivia was now trapped between the two of them. Adolphus, not quite sure what was going on, had been sniffing around the boys' feet, but he now decided they were friends and went to hunt woodlice in the corner, waving his tail happily.

"Well, okay," said Olivia, trying not to sound bothered. "What do you want to know?"

"I want to know where your dratted brother is and what spell he's cooking up for tomorrow. I want to know exactly what spell, because I want to make sure it doesn't win. And to make a counter-charm I need to know what it's for, see?" said Snotty nastily, putting his face close to Olivia's and waving the frog in front of her.

Max, despite being held in a pincer grip, wriggled his back legs in outrage. No wonder his bucket spell hadn't worked last year! Snotty Hogsbottom had been operating a counter-charm. The dirty rotten cheating scumbag!

"I'm not telling you!" said Olivia, hotly. "You horrible cheat! Why should I sneak on my own brother?"

"Because," said Snotty meaningfully, "If you don't, I shall be forced to drop your frog into the moat. And I've heard there's a six-foot-long pike in it."

He moved to the window and held his arm out over the water. Olivia could see Max shaking his frog head frantically. But did that mean, 'No, don't tell him, I'd rather die!' or 'No, don't let him drop me in the moat, tell him everything, I'm not proud'?

Olivia sighed.

"All right, you win. He's planning to turn me—"

The frog croaked loudly, and frantically waved its back legs.

"Purple," finished Olivia, and Max sighed

with relief. But not for long.

"Purple?" laughed Snotty. "What a loser! That's the easiest spell in the book. I guess he really doesn't have any ambition, after all. Well, thanks," he added carelessly, and opened his finger and thumb so that the small orange frog dropped like a stone to the grey water fifty feet below.

"You cheating toadwart!" yelled Olivia, hurling herself at Snotty, but Jerome had her pinned to the wall quicker than you could say 'drowned frog' and Snotty walked calmly past her with a chuckle.

"Oh dear, my hand slipped. But what a fuss about an old frog. Plenty more in the castle duck pond."

As he passed her, Snotty sprinkled around a few drops of liquid from a flask hanging from his belt and Olivia found herself completely unable to move a muscle in her arms or legs. She slid down the wall to a sitting position with a thump as the two boys strolled from the room, laughing loudly.

"Come on Jerome," she heard Snotty say as they shut the door with a loud thud, "Need to do some sword practice and then it'll be time to get that brat away from the castle for Father."

Encounter with a Wizard

The moat was extremely deep and very murky.
Max entered it head first, having completely
lost any sense of what was up and what was down as
he tumbled, with flailing arms and legs, down from
the window. At first he panicked that he couldn't
breathe, but then he remembered that he was a frog
and wouldn't need air for ages, so he relaxed. He
stopped sinking and started to float gently back up

through the water. Not only was he not dead, he realised, but it was actually quite pleasant down here. He couldn't see very far in the greenish gloom, but there were a few small silvery fish swimming nearby and not far from where he was floating, he could just make out the outline of the castle wall

Max swam up to the stone wall and considered the situation. It was vertical and very smooth. He tried pushing his feet up against it, but they just slipped and propelled him backwards into the murky gloom. He swam a little further, looking for a crack between stones. He found one that looked quite deep and promising and stuck a front leg in, hoping to get enough of a grip to pull himself up.

Ow!

Something in the crack had bitten him! Max peered in and saw what looked like an angry crayfish waving its long pincers at him. He hurriedly moved on. This was getting a bit serious. He could try the other side, but that was just the same, and at the surface he'd find himself outside the castle without any prospect of crawling back in through a window to find Olivia and the antidote.

Suddenly, Max heard a strange whooshing noise and a cloud of small fish whizzed past him, swimming as if their lives depended on it. Then Max realised that that was probably because their lives did depend on it. Ripples of water followed them and a huge, ominous, dark shape started to emerge from the gloom. Snotty's words as he had held him out over the moat came back to him with crystal clarity: "I've heard there's a six-foot-long pike in it..." Pike, as Max knew very well, are savage hunters – big, mean, freshwater predator fish, the river's equivalent of the Great White Shark. Big ones like this could swallow a frog in one mouthful.

He dived, hoping desperately that the pike would be too interested in the shoal of fish to notice one small frog. Unfortunately, the movement caught the pike's attention and it turned, cast around a little for the scent and then dived after him.

Olivia was boiling with rage, but she couldn't do anything about it. She appeared to be completely immobilised. She could, however, talk.

"Ferocious!" she yelled. "Where are you, you good-for-nothing useless coward? Why didn't you bite their ankles or something?! Adolphus! You are the most soft-headed dragon that ever lived! Go and singe their eyebrows off!"

"Oh, sorry!" said Adolphus, bounding up from the corner where he'd been chasing woodlice. "Did you need me?"

Ferocious emerged yawning from behind the tapestry.

"Did someone call my name?"

"Yes!" said Olivia crossly. "Max has been chucked in the moat by Snotty Hogsbottom and I can't move a muscle because he put a spell on me on the way out."

"Ah," said Ferocious, sagely. "Things not going so well, then."

"Ferocious! You'll have to jump in the moat and go after Max. Adolphus can't because he wouldn't fit though these windows."

"And I'm afraid of heights," added Adolphus happily.

"See if you can find him before the pike does. Then both of you need to find your way back here to get the antidote."

"Oh, not much to ask, then," said Ferocious, wrinkling up his nose. "Just leap into pike-infested waters, somehow extract a small orange frog and escort him up to the fourth floor of the castle without being stepped on. Always the way, isn't it? Good old Ferocious to the rescue. Off we go again, risking life and limb. Ho hum." Nevertheless, he scrabbled up to the window and launched himself out into the air, landing in the moat a few seconds later with loud plop.

"Well," said Olivia. "Let's hope he finds Max and that neither of them gets eaten by the pike. Now we just need to think of a plan to get me unstuck.

I wonder – Adolphus, can you get at the green bottle with the reversal potion?"

Adolphus bounded up happily and looked all around eagerly.

"Green bottle? Yes, yes, I'll get it. Adolphus to the rescue – whoopee! Potion in a bottle, umm – bottle spell – er – can't see it... Sorry, what colour did you say?"

But at that moment, the heavy oak door to the room creaked open and a tall, fierce-looking man wearing a long grey cloak walked in and then stopped in surprise.

"Dragon's teeth! What are you doing in my room, young lady?"

"Um, sorry," said Olivia, trying hard to sit up straighter but not moving a muscle. "I didn't realise it was your room, your worshipfulness."

"No, sorry, sorry, sorry," said Adolphus, equally in awe of the forbidding-looking man.

The man looked at them both very hard, then sat down on a large oak chair by the door. His dark chestnut-brown hair had streaks of grey and there were lines round his eyes, but his look was bright and fierce, like a bird's. Under the cloak he was wearing dark leggings and a grey tunic, and he had a long sword attached to a plain wide leather belt.

"Well," he said at last. "It appears that you've been enchanted, young lady, so before we do anything else, I'd better release you."

He gestured towards her with the long elegant fingers of his right hand and suddenly Olivia found she could move. She stood up and curtsied gratefully, and the man nodded in acknowledgement.

"Now. Perhaps I'd better introduce myself. I am Merlin and this is my room. Usually, I lock it. I'm rather surprised you managed to get in. Did you come by yourself?"

"No, my lord," said Olivia. Merlin didn't look anything like she had always imagined him. In fact, come to think of it, she was sure she had seen this tall, fierce-looking man before, but had always assumed he was one of the king's many knights. "I came with my brother, Max. We had no idea it was your room. We wanted somewhere to practise for the competition tomorrow."

"Ah. So your brother is a novice," said Merlin thoughtfully. "And you are?"

"Lady Olivia Pendragon. And this is Adolphus."

"Pleased to meet you," said Merlin to both of them. "Now. If you were enchanted into immobility, I'm assuming something rather nastier happened to your brother?"

"Er, well, he was a frog," said Olivia uncertainly.

"He was turned into a frog?" said Merlin, his eyebrows shooting up.

"Well, not exactly," said Olivia, wringing her hands and wondering how much to tell the wizard. She looked up at his piercing grey eyes and decided that truth was probably the best policy. "He invented a spell to turn people into frogs," she said hurriedly. "And we were practising it. Then Snotty

– er – Adrian Hogsbottom came in and threw him in the moat, not realising he was Max – and magicked me so I couldn't go and tell on him. And please, we really need to try to find him, if he hasn't been eaten by the pike. And now Ferocious is down there too – that's Max's pet rat. I really hope they're all right!"

To Olivia's annoyance, she found she was on the verge of tears and her voice had gone all high and squeaky. Adolphus licked her hand comfortingly. She took a deep breath and looked at Merlin. He was looking very thoughtful, sitting in the great chair with his chin on his hands.

"Interesting," he mused, almost to himself. "A frogspell. Of course, the Pendragons are a very magical family all in all. Well, well. I shall have to meet young Max. I shall definitely have to meet him. But we must find him first."

He rose and went to the window that looked down on the grey waters of the moat. "Now—"

He was interrupted by a loud banging on the

door, which was opened almost immediately. Olivia gasped as she realised that the man who had burst in was the king! Arthur was tall, with dark, straight hair and a worried, careworn look. He glanced at her distractedly, then went straight to Merlin.

"Merlin!" he said urgently. "The prince has gone missing! We've looked through all of his quarters – Sir Gareth is searching the rest of the castle now – but he's just vanished! We thought he was with his mother, his mother thought he was with his nurse – it seems no one's seen him since early morning!"

Merlin frowned. "Who knows that he's missing?"

"Myself, Sir Gareth – you... His mother's been told he's playing with Sir Gareth's boys – and we have to keep it that way. If it gets out he's missing..."

"It'll be war," said Merlin grimly. "We need to keep this to ourselves. We can't raise the alarm, or even alert the guards. But we'll find him – he must be in the castle. I set up a spell around the walls for protection and there's no one who could break that enchantment, except—" He hesitated, and then shrugged. "Your sister, the Lady Morgana le Fay – when is she due?"

Arthur raised his eyebrows. "This evening, I believe. But why? Might we need her help, do you think?"

Merlin laughed shortly. "I hope not. I think I'll do my best to find the prince before she arrives, my lord. But we need to hurry."

Arthur nodded, and strode out of the room, and Merlin turned gravely to Olivia. "I'm afraid you'll have to search for your brother yourself, my lady. Good luck! But I must warn you – you are not to tell anyone about what you have heard here. We don't want this news to reach the wrong ears. So not a word!" He gave her a stern look, then swept out of the room after the king, shutting the door behind him with a thud.

Olivia stood for a moment, looking thoughtful.

"Adolphus?" she said at last. "Do you remember Snotty saying something about getting the brat away from the castle?"

Schemes and Enchantments

Max swam faster than he thought it was possible for a small orange frog to swim, but the pike was faster. Within seconds, he could almost feel the tip of its nose inches from his back legs and its mean-looking jaws opening wide, ready to snap shut and swallow him whole...

Max was seconds away from being a tasty pike snack when he spotted a deep crevice between the stones of the wall to his left. He swerved into the narrow, dark space and kicked frantically to propel himself as far up it as possible. If there was a crayfish in this one, thought Max, it could just share or he'd poke its eyes out.

He had just whipped his back legs into the crack, when the pike's jaws hit the wall with a thud and he saw its sharp teeth scraping across the stones, trying to prise him away from the wall. Max gulped and pushed himself as far into the crevice as he could. The pike circled for a while, coming back to investigate, trying to sniff out where that annoying little creature had disappeared to, but eventually it got bored and glided off in search of easier prey.

Phew!

Max looked around and saw that this really was a very deep crevice. It seemed to continue into the wall. He swam forward, then realised he would have to climb, as a large square stone blocked the way. Max clambered up the edge of the stone and then saw another gap leading back deeper into the wall. It looked as if he might be able to crawl all the way through to the castle.

Slowly, carefully, Max pulled himself up and through the gaps in the thick stone walls. In places the stones were set so tight he could only just squeeze through, feeling like his eyeballs were going to pop out. In other places deep, dark crevices seemed to reach back into the wall for miles and smelled like something horrible lived in them. Max hopped past these as fast as he could. He was gradually climbing higher, well above the level of the moat now, and it was beginning to feel as if he'd been crawling forever. He remembered once hearing someone say that the walls of the castle were thick enough to have whole rooms hidden in them, and he could believe it now. It was hot in the wall, and difficult to breathe – he could feel the weight of the hundreds of stones above him and couldn't help picturing what a very squished frog he would be if any of them slipped.

At last the darkness around him started to

seem a little less black, and then distinctly grey, and soon after that he began to see glimpses of brightness in between the cracks. Max squeezed through a particularly small gap and realised that he was now behind the very last layer of stones. They were cut squarer and more neatly than the others and, he realised with a sinking feeling, they were much more closely fitted together – it was going to be difficult to get out into the room beyond. Max scanned up and down and sideways for a bigger gap, and then with huge relief he saw light streaming in. The corner of one of the stones was broken off! He scrambled over to it and peered cautiously into the chamber beyond.

It was a medium-sized room, square and quite richly furnished – a knight's quarters, Max guessed. There were tapestries on the walls and a rich embroidered carpet on the floor. Two large windows allowed light into the chamber. There didn't appear to be anyone there. After a few minutes of waiting for noises Max carefully eased himself out of the

wall and fell, plop, onto the carpet. He breathed a
sigh of relief. He'd done it! He'd managed to escape
the moat and the pike, and he'd got back into the
castle – now all he had to do was find Olivia and get
turned back into a boy.

Max scanned the room quickly for the way
out. In one corner was a small arched recess, which
probably led to the toilet. That wasn't going to get
him anywhere except down a long smelly chute to
the moat again... The archway in the opposite wall
looked more promising, but as Max started to hop
towards it, he heard voices in the corridor outside,
and a door started to open. Quickly he leapt to the
shelter of the wall and hid in the shadow of one of
the trailing tapestries.

***

Sir Richard Hogsbottom was trying his very best to
be ingratiating, and his very best was very good
indeed, since he was famous in Camelot for being
the biggest bootlicker that ever lived. His plump
red face was positively glistening with the effort

of sucking up to the lady by his side, and it seemed that even his robes curved round his ample body in a humble and admiring sort of way.

"My lady," he was saying, as he ushered his companion into his chambers with what he hoped a winning and loyal smile (he actually looked like he had swallowed a boot). "Permit me to welcome you to my humble chambers – I apologise that I have no food or drink to offer that is worthy of your attention but perhaps a little—"

His companion held up her hand for silence. She was a tall, slim woman with long black hair and pale skin. She was beautiful, but she looked like a marble statue, with no real life or warmth in her expression. Her eyes were such a pale blue that they were almost colourless. She stopped dead in the centre of the room and turned her head, frowning in concentration, almost tasting the air around her.

"Magic," she said, her pale eyes sweeping over the rich tapestries on the walls and the embroidered carpet under her feet. "There's something magic in the room." Her voice was as smooth as honey, low and silky, but it made Max shudder. He cowered closer to the wall as he felt her eyes pass across the place where he was hiding. "Something... Has the door been locked while you were out, Sir Richard?"

"Why yes, of course, my lady, completely locked," protested Sir Richard, looking anxious. "But perhaps – you know, Merlin is working every hour of the day and night to make sure nothing happens to the prince... Is it possible a small checking spell may have crept under the door?"

"Mmm..." said the lady, considering the situation. Then she laughed and it was like the tinkling of icicles falling on hard frost. "Merlin – of course – sniffing around the castle, trying to find out what's up. He's going to get a shock when he finds his spell wall broken and the prince gone! Ha! Then he'll have to kneel before me and beg for help, and then..." she lowered her voice, but Max, cowering in the tapestries beside her, could just hear her say to herself in a bleak and savage whisper, "Then we'll see King Arthur broken!"

* * *

Adolphus flew silently down the long, dark corridor and settled as quietly as possible on the roof beams near the end. Beneath him, two boys were squabbling.

"I'm not doing it, Adrian, I'm not, it's too dangerous! Merlin's on the prowl now and he'll find us out for sure. He's bound to!"

"Don't be such a coward, Jerome!" hissed the other boy. "There's been no alarm raised, the guards don't know anything. No one's going to bother with two young squires going out for a ride in the middle of all this bustle for the festival."

"But what if the brat wakes up and starts yelling?"

"I told you," said Snotty scornfully. "I'll have a full immobility spell on him. He's not going to be moving a muscle or saying anything, never mind yelling. Just buck up, Jerome! Druid's toenails! All we have to do is roll him up in a blanket on the back of one of our horses and then we stroll out of the castle. If they ask, we tell them we're taking provisions to one of the camps. Come on!"

Snotty tried to pull Jerome down the next passage, but Jerome's plump face was still looking rather pale and he obstinately refused to move.

"What about the spell wall?" he said stubbornly.

"I told you!" said Snotty, exasperated. "She's dealt with it. It won't be a problem."

"You mean Lady—"

"Shhh! Don't even think about saying her name! She has ways of dealing with traitors you don't even want to hear about!"

Jerome looked distinctly mutinous, but after a few moments he shrugged. "Okay. If you say so. But I've heard Merlin can turn people into dung beetles and I really don't fancy having six legs and living on a pile of horse manure for the rest of my life."

The two boys set off down the passage

towards the stables. As they disappeared, Adolphus looked back down the corridor and beckoned with a claw. Olivia, pressing herself against the wall, eased herself quietly along until she reached the dragon. She was wearing a pair of Max's leggings and a dark tunic, and with her dark hair and some smudgy dirt on her face, blended very well into the shadows.

"I told you, Adolphus!" she whispered excitedly. "I knew those two had something to do with it!"

"Shall we follow them some more?" said Adolphus, jumping up and down on the beam. "I can be really really quiet again. I can see where they're going."

"I don't know..." said Olivia, thinking – but she was too late. Adolphus, twirling his wings, was off in a flash of blue-green scales and she was forced to go after him.

As they turned the corner, they saw that the passageway was empty. Adolphus started to fly round in circles anxiously. "Where are they?

We need to catch them! Where have they gone?!" he twittered.

"Adolphus!" Olivia hissed. "Wait! Come back! I think it might be better if we just go and find Merlin!"

"Yes, it probably would be better," drawled a familiar voice, and Snotty stepped out from a dark shadowy doorway behind her. "But I don't think we'll be letting you, actually. Not so great for us, you see."

"Snotty!" groaned Olivia. "Oh dungballs!"

"Dungballs indeed, my dearest Olivia," said Snotty as he forced one of her arms up behind her back and Jerome emerged from the gloom to grab the other one. "I thought I'd sorted you out once already today... You know, if you're going to go sneaking around and poking your nose in where it's not wanted, you really shouldn't do it with a pea-brained pet dragon who sounds like a herd of griffins stalking down the corridor. We could have heard you three counties away."

He turned and threw a handful of something at Adolphus, who was flapping around their heads in a flurry of wings and anxiety, and the dragon dropped to the ground like a stone.

Kidnapped!

Sir Richard Hogsbottom was rubbing his plump hands in glee. Lady Morgana le Fay, the most powerful enchantress in the land, half-sister to the king himself, was in his chambers, drinking his best vintage Roman wine and talking to him like an equal. Well, almost like an equal. Okay, so he had to stand, while she sat in the big carved oak chair. And she told him what to do, while he said "Yes, my lady" and "No, my lady" – but they were in the same room! And he was in on the plot! He was a trusted co-conspirator in her plan to topple King Arthur!

Sir Richard smiled to himself. He'd been quite surprised to find how much she hated her half-brother, how strongly she wanted to replace him and be queen. She did such a good job of appearing adoring, most of the time. But now he knew the truth. And when his son Adrian had done his bit, he, Sir Richard, was going to be the new queen's favourite. Rich, famous – why, he could have that awful Sir Bertram Pendragon hung from the castle walls by his toenails if he wanted. And he would certainly get bigger and more richly furnished rooms when he stayed in Camelot – this one was poky, and there was a distinct smell of pondweed coming from somewhere...

"Sir Richard!" Lady Morgana's voice brought him back from his daydreaming with a start.

"Indeed, my lady, indeed, yes, I agree absolutely!" he stuttered, not sure what she had been talking about.

"I said, when is your son expected?" said Lady Morgana, coldly.

"Oh, er, yes, sorry, indeed – well, any minute now, your graciousness. Should be along directly. Very good boy, Adrian, very clever – quite a dab hand at magic himself, you know, won the Novices' two years running!"

Behind the tapestry, Max was seething. Snotty Hogsbottom! It wasn't his magic skills – it was his cheating, lying, weasel skills that had won him the Novices' two years running. It wasn't going to happen again. Assuming, of course, that Max could escape, find Olivia and be ready for the competition tomorrow afternoon. Right now, that seemed trickier than it had before Sir Richard and Lady Morgana had entered the room. And it was about to get even trickier.

Sir Richard's 'proud father' act was interrupted by a loud bang at the door. Almost instantly it flew open to reveal Snotty, holding a struggling, kicking Olivia, while Jerome stood behind them, staggering under the dead weight of a small blue-green dragon, who was out cold.

"Adrian!" spluttered Sir Richard. "What's going on? What on earth? What's she doing here?"

Olivia tried to speak, but they had gagged her with a tunic belt and all she could manage was, "Mmmnph... Mmmnph!"

Snotty shoved her viciously and she fell to the ground in a sprawl of limbs in front of Lady Morgana, who looked down at her as if she were a particularly slimy kind of slug.

"It's that weed Pendragon's little sister," Snotty spat. "Lurking around after us with her dung-brained pet dragon. They heard me talking to Jerome about taking the prince out to the forest... We've got to get rid of them."

"Oh, er, well, that's rather extreme, surely? Perhaps if we just, well, er – my lady?" Sir Richard turned to Lady Morgana with a slightly appalled expression on his plump face. He really hadn't banked on anyone having to get hurt in this escapade. Humiliated, yes. Brought to the brink of war, fine. Deposed and thrown in the dungeon while everyone else feasted and celebrated, only what was to be expected. But got rid of? Actual bodily harm? He wasn't really made for that kind of thing...

"Not just yet," said Lady Morgana decisively. "She may be useful as an extra hostage. If not, we can deal with her later. For now, I think it is time we got on with the plan. Leave the girl and the dragon here and lock the door. They won't be going anywhere." She laughed, and on the floor Olivia shivered at the sound.

"Come along, Sir Richard – we need to go and help the boys get their horses 'packed', don't we?" And she swept out of the room with Snotty at her side and Sir Richard, feeling rather weak at the knees, following. Jerome dumped Adolphus on the floor and headed out after them.

The door thudded shut and Max heard the key being turned in the lock.

"Olivia!" he croaked. "Olivia! I'm here, by the tapestries..." He hopped towards his sister, who was picking herself up off the floor.

"Mmmmnph! Mmmmnph!" she said excitedly when she saw the orange frog hopping towards her. "Mmmnph... Mmmnph!" She reached up and clumsily pulled at the gag, eventually managing to drag it off, half undone.

"Phew, that's better! Max! How did you end up here?"

"Well," said Max, taking a deep breath. He was about to embark on a long and detailed explanation of his trials and tribulations in the moat and inside the castle walls when they were both distracted by a rustling sound, followed by a loud squeak, and a muffled curse. With that, a large black rat squeezed its way out of a gap in the stone wall and fell to the ground with a thud.

"All right, all right, you can stop panicking, I've made it, I'm in one piece, just about, though I do think I may have rather less fur than I had at the beginning... And I'm not sure that pike didn't have a tiny bit of the end of my tail, but still, never mind, can't complain, all in a day's work." Ferocious looked around, and noticed Olivia, and then Adolphus sprawled unconscious on the floor. "Well, well, all here together," he added. "Isn't that nice?"

"Ferocious!" exclaimed Max happily. "You came after me!"

"Well, I didn't have a lot of choice really," said Ferocious, modestly. "Seeing as your sister more or less threw me out the window... Go and rescue Max, she says. Oh yes, piece of cake, say I, no problem, just follow the smell of pondweed. You can rely on good old Ferocious to brave terrible pikes and—"

But Max and Olivia had stopped listening. They were too busy exchanging news and piecing together the bits of plot they had overheard between them.

"Ah, well," sighed Ferocious. "Always the way. No gratitude." And he started to clean his whiskers and check how much fur he had lost in the castle walls.

"So," said Max thoughtfully. "They're heading off now, on horseback?"

"Yes," said Olivia. "Snotty will have the prince wrapped in blankets on his horse – Lady Morgana has sorted Merlin's spell wall so it won't be a problem – and they said, they were taking him to the forest. They must mean Grimeswood – it's about five miles away downriver. But the forest is huge. No one will find them if they've got a hiding place in there somewhere."

"We need to stop them before they leave the castle," said Max.

"But we can't get a message to anyone," objected Olivia. "The only way out of here is down the toilet or out of the window!"

"Hmm," said Max. "I'm not keen on the toilet. But out of the window..."

"You're a frog, Max, you don't have wings," said Olivia.

"I haven't got wings," said Max. "But he has..."

and he pointed one webbed foot at Adolphus, sprawled on the carpet, before shouting, "Ferocious!"

"Oh, decided to remember I exist, have you?" said Ferocious brightly. "Want something done, I expect."

"Yes," said Max. "Go and bite Adolphus and see if you can wake him up from whatever enchantment he's got on him."

"Pleasure," said Ferocious, baring his teeth in an evil grin and scampering over to the dragon.

"Oh, don't hurt him too much," begged Olivia, but Ferocious was being quite gentle, nipping Adolphus on the ears and nuzzling his head, while Max shook him hard and tried to lift up his eyelids.

It seemed to be working. Adolphus snuffled and moved a leg, then opened one eye blearily.

"Wh-wh-wh- what? Wassamatter? Wha' goin' on?" he said, shaking his head and snorting a small breath of fire that just missed scorching Ferocious' tail. "Wh-who? Wh-where? Not for breakfast, thank you. What? No. Woodlice!"

"Hopeless," said Ferocious, sadly. "He never did have much up there but the spell must have addled his brains completely."

Adolphus stood up, staggered, shook himself and opened both eyes.

"Brrr!" he said, breathing a burst of fire, before he looked around. "Olivia! Max! Ferocious! We're all together! Whoopee, what fun! What are we doing?"

"Ah well," said Ferocious. "Back to the usual level of brainlessness, then. It's a start."

"Adolphus!" said Olivia delightedly, giving the dragon a big hug. "I was worried about you! You got zapped by Snotty's spell and we weren't sure we could wake you up. We're all trapped in Sir Richard Hogsbottom's chambers and we need you to fly out of the window and get help!"

"Oh, right, okay! Good! Rescue, yes! What fun!" said Adolphus. He bounced up to the window and peered out.

"Oh. Er. It's rather high up, isn't it?" he said in a small voice.

"Oh, Adolphus!" groaned Olivia. "You are hopeless. How can a dragon be scared of heights? We're only on the second floor!"

Max hopped up to the wall by the window.

"Lift me up," he croaked at Olivia. "I want to see where we are."

She picked him up carefully and put him in the window recess next to Adolphus. Max hopped to the edge and looked out.

"I can see the drawbridge!" he said. "We're at the front of the castle. And we aren't that high. Come on, Adolphus, it's not that bad!"

"Oh, well... er..." said Adolphus warily, reaching one claw out of the window and then drawing it back hurriedly. "Actually, I don't feel very well..."

"Oh no! Olivia! I can see Snotty!" shrieked Max suddenly, hopping up and down on the spot. "He's got his horse – he's with Jerome – they're talking to the castle gate guards! He's going to get away!"

"Where?" said Olivia, peering on tiptoe out of the window. Then she saw them. "Oh, no!" she groaned. "We'll never be able to get a message to anyone before they've gone!"

"Oh, what are we going to do?" wailed Max in an agony of impatience. "We'll never stop them, and we can't follow them and find out where they go because we don't have horses and anyway they'd see us on horses and – oh! I've got it!" he smacked his head with one webbed foot. "Why didn't I think of it before?! Adolphus, you have to fly out of the window and you're going to have to take me with you! We can fly after them and rescue the prince ourselves!"

"Brilliant!" exclaimed Olivia. "Adolphus can carry you in his claws! And he won't be scared if he's got you with him, will you, Adolphus?"

"Er, well, umm... maybe not quite so much," said Adolphus nervously.

"Good idea, Max," said Ferocious, jumping up onto the ledge beside them. "Excellent. And when you get to where they've taken the prince, you can hop over to Snotty Hogsbottom and slap him senseless with your webbed feet."

Max considered this. "I guess it probably wouldn't be so good trying to rescue the prince when I'm still a frog," he admitted.

"But Max," said Olivia excitedly. "I've still got the antidote potion! You can turn yourself back when you get there!"

"Brilliant!" said Max. "Although I think I might try to avoid any actual confrontation, even if I am turned back. I'm sure there'll be a way to rescue the prince without any actual fighting..." He coughed, and avoided Olivia's eye.

She reached down the front of her tunic and brought out the potion bottle with the frogspell antidote. "Here," she said. "You'd better hurry. Take Ferocious, he's good in a scrap. And he can hold the potion bottle in his teeth."

She passed it over to Ferocious, who sighed and took it carefully.

"Hold tight, Ferocious," said Olivia, and then grinned. "Actually, I've just thought – even if he drops the potion bottle, you could always get him or Adolphus to kiss you back."

Max shuddered. "Hold on to that bottle for dear life, Ferocious," he said.

"Don't worry," said Ferocious. "I intend to."

Max suddenly realised that this plan meant leaving Olivia on her own, trapped in Sir Richard's chambers, with Morgana's threats still hanging over her head. Olivia seemed to have realised this at the same moment. They stared at each other.

"Er – perhaps I should just find someone to come and rescue you, rather than going after Snotty," said Max, looking worried.

Olivia gulped. "No, it's okay," she said, thinking of Arthur and how worried he'd looked. "I'll be all right. Find the prince, Max, and you can rescue me afterwards."

"Right, then," said Max. "Come on, Adolphus, Ferocious. Olivia – we'll make sure someone gets to you before anything awful happens, I promise."

"Yes, OK, Max," she said in a small voice, and then leaned over to kiss him goodbye.

"Noooooo!" shrieked Max, and she stopped just in time.

"Oh, yes!" she said, laughing shakily. "I forgot. Good luck all of you! Better go, quick!"

Max peered out of the window and saw Snotty and Jerome cantering across the drawbridge and down the road to the river. He hopped over to Adolphus, who picked him up in one claw, while Ferocious jumped onto the dragon's back and dug his claws in.

"Okay," he said. "Adolphus – go!"

"Aaaaarrghhh!" wailed Adolphus, and shutting his eyes he launched himself off the window ledge and started to flap his wings like crazy as he plummeted like a stone towards the moat below.

A Knockout Punch

Max, Ferocious and Adolphus were perched uncomfortably in the upper branches of a large oak tree in Grimeswood Forest. After his spectacular skydive almost to the surface of the moat, Adolphus had suddenly remembered how wings work. He'd corrected his downward plunge with a tremendous jerk, soaring over the heads of the startled castle guards while Max and Ferocious tried hard not to be sick. Then they had glided for miles over the countryside, always keeping Snotty and Jerome in sight, until they reached the edge of Grimeswood. It was gloomy in the forest, with the closeness of the trees blotting out most of the bright midday sun, and they had had to follow more closely for the last hour, flying carefully from tree to tree. Now, however, it seemed that Snotty and Jerome had at last reached their destination: a small stone hut, deep among the trees.

"I don't like it, Adrian," Jerome was saying nervously, looking over his shoulder. "I'm sure we're being followed."

"Oh, stop moaning, Jerome!" said Snotty impatiently. "Druid's toenails! Remind me never to attempt any dark and dangerous deeds with you in tow again, you're such a wimp! Here, help me with the prince!"

Reluctantly Jerome came and took one end of the bundle Snotty was pulling off his horse, and they staggered into the hut and shut the door.

"Ferocious!" hissed Max. "Change me back! I might be able to get the horses away while they're in there!"

Ferocious quickly pulled the bottle stopper out with his teeth and shook a few drops of potion onto the orange frog in front of him. There was a flash, followed by a loud crack. The branch Max had been sitting on quite happily as a frog suddenly snapped under the weight of an eleven-year-old boy and he fell to the forest floor like a stunned dragon.

"Oww! Dungballs!" he swore, as he rolled over on the ground and then staggered to his knees. He quickly glanced over at the hut, but all seemed quiet there still. He looked up at the tree.

"Ferocious! Adolphus!" he called quietly. "Come down! I might need backup."

There was a scramble as the two of them appeared, peering through the lower canopy of leaves. Ferocious leaped down onto Max's shoulder and nipped his ear affectionately.

"I do prefer you when you're a boy, Max,"

he said happily. 'You smell so awful when you're a frog.'

Max grinned and tickled the rat behind his ears, where he liked it. "Come on," he said, "let's see if we can get these horses away..."

He tiptoed over to where the horses were grazing and then stopped. Horses made him nervous at the best of times and these were rather large. He reached out a tentative hand towards the nearest one, which looked up and snorted at him. Max took a hurried step backwards. The horse moved closer, trying to nibble at his tunic.

"Good horse," said Max, not sounding very convincing. "Good horse – er – just go away, will you? Shoo!"

Just as Max thought he was going to have to leg it, Adolphus shot out of the tree and swooped down on them, breathing fire. The horse jerked its head up and whinnied in terror. In the twitch of a dragon's tail, the two horses had crashed off down the forest path as fast as their legs would take them.

Adolphus flew triumphantly in circles round Max's head.

"Did you see that? Did you see them go? Whoosh! I just breathed a little fire and, hey, gone! Hurrah for Adolphus!"

"Fantastic, Adolphus, very good," said Max hurriedly. "But for goodness' sake, hide!" and he dived behind a bush just as Snotty and Jerome appeared wide-eyed at the door of the hut.

"What was that?" shouted Jerome in a panic. "Where have the horses gone? I told you we'd been followed!"

"Shut up!" said Snotty savagely. "I don't know what it was, but the horses have bolted. We'd better try and get them back or Father'll be furious when he gets here with her."

"I don't want—" began Jerome but Snotty cut him off.

"You don't want to have to share a horse's back with Lady Morgana, Jerome, believe me. And if we have to share, I'm going with Father."

This was enough to silence Jerome, who nervously followed Snotty down the forest path after the horses.

"Quick!" whispered Max to the others. "Into the hut!"

As Snotty and Jerome disappeared off into the gloom, Max, Adolphus and Ferocious crept into the small hut. There was a faint yellow light from a lamp hanging from the ceiling, and by it Max could see a small boy, lying on a wooden bed in the corner of the room and looking rather haughtily at them. He was about seven years old, and rather pale and grubby, but Max could see that his clothes were very rich indeed and he had an air of being used to getting his own way.

"We've come to rescue you," said Max. "Can you move? Has the immobility spell worn off?"

"You're not a very big rescuer," the boy said. "I think the spell's worn off a bit, but I can't move my legs. Are you a wizard?"

"Well, a bit of one," said Max, modestly.

"That's how we managed to get here and find you. But I don't know enough to reverse the spell. We'll just have to help you till it wears off."

"I wasn't thinking of the spell," said the boy. "I just thought you might need a spell for them," and he pointed at the door.

Max turned. There stood Jerome, looking wide and meaty, and Snotty, with his arms crossed and a sneer on his face.

Adolphus launched himself at Snotty, breathing fire, but the boy just laughed nastily and sidestepped, at the same time throwing some powder at Adolphus. At once the dragon found his flames had turned pink and were now just faintly warm and tickly.

"Oww! That's cheating!" squealed Adolphus, but Snotty couldn't understand dragon and wouldn't have cared if he could. He stalked further into the room, leaving the way clear for Adolphus to deal with Jerome, Max saw with relief. Even with lukewarm fire, the small dragon was a whirl of blue-green, flashing scales and claws and teeth, and Jerome fled yelling, with Adolphus chasing him down the path.

"Well, well, what on earth are you doing here?" Snotty drawled, looking Max up and down contemptuously.

"I might ask you the same thing," said Max, trying to sound braver than he felt.

Snotty Hogsbottom sneered.

"I'm doing a job for an important person – and she won't want you sticking your nose in. You're dead meat, Pendragon. You'd better start saying your prayers."

Max swallowed. Snotty was a lot bigger and heavier than he was and Max didn't think having Ferocious there to bite his ankles was going to even up the odds enough. But he wasn't going to give up without a fight. He tried to remember all the things his father had told him about hand to hand combat. He wished he'd paid a bit more attention in boxing classes. He wished he wasn't so small. He wished he had bigger biceps...

Measuring up the distance to Snotty's face, Max recalled one piece of useful advice from Sir Bertram: "Straight on the nose, son, when they're least expecting it. Put your whole body into it!"

Snotty was reaching into his jacket and starting to pull out a potion bottle. It was now or never. Max launched himself, kicking off with his legs, throwing his arm forward and following it with his shoulder, aiming his fist right at the centre of Snotty's surprised-looking face.

WHAM!

His fist completely missed Snotty's face, but the force of his charge carried him straight on and sent the bigger boy flying. Snotty's head hit the stone wall of the hut with a crack! and he slumped to the floor like a sack of corn.

Max scrambled up from the floor and looked down at Snotty. He had gone a slightly funny colour and he appeared to be completely out for the count, but he was still breathing.

"Wow!" said the prince, in awe. "That was amazing!"

"Yes, well done, Max," said Ferocious, sitting on Snotty's stomach and calmly cleaning his whiskers. "Of course, you couldn't have done it without me distracting him with a few well-aimed nips to the ankles, but still – your father would be proud of you."

Max took a deep breath. He couldn't quite believe what had happened. He'd knocked Snotty out cold and Adolphus had chased Jerome goodness knows where – it looked as if he'd actually rescued the prince. He was in charge! Max suddenly felt rather weak and sat down quickly before his knees gave way.

At that moment Adolphus flew happily through the doorway, breathing proper-coloured fire again and flapping excitedly around their heads.

"I chased him off! All the way down the path! Did you see? He found one of the horses in the end and galloped off in completely the wrong direction for the castle! It was really good fun! Did you see me breathe a really big bit of flame just now? Whoopee!"

"Yes, well done, Adolphus," said Ferocious hurriedly. "Just calm down before you set the place alight. That would be all we need – heroes of the hour burned to a crisp by their brainless companion."

Adolphus flew down to the ground and folded his wings, but he couldn't stop bouncing. "Now what, Max? What shall I do now? What do you want me to do, Max? Shall I breathe fire again? Just let me know!"

Max took a deep breath, and looked round the hut. "Um, actually, you could breath some fire over here, Adolphus," he said, showing the dragon the fireplace where Snotty and Jerome had laid a neat little pile of logs and twigs, just ready to light. "I'm going to tie Snotty up, in case he comes round, but I think we all need something to warm us up. Plus I'm starving. I don't know about you lot, but being scared makes me really hungry."

"No problem!" said Adolphus, and sent a three-foot flame scorching into the narrow fireplace and halfway up the chimney. At once, the logs glowed red hot and started to crackle merrily. Meanwhile, Max trussed Snotty up like a chicken ready for the oven and Ferocious sniffed about in Snotty and Jerome's saddlebags for food and drink. In what seemed like no time, the prince and his rescuers were sitting happily by the fire, drinking hot spiced apple juice and eating bread and cheese. The young prince was much friendlier than he'd been when they'd first appeared. He couldn't understand a word Ferocious or Adolphus said, but Max translated, and he solemnly thanked all of them for what they had done.

"You can call me Cael, if you like," he said rather grandly. "After all, you are my rescuers."

"Well, I suppose technically we haven't rescued you till we get you back to the castle," said Max – and then suddenly he felt cold all over.

Olivia! Olivia was still in the castle, still trapped in Sir Richard's rooms, and possibly at the mercy of Morgana at this very moment! What had he been thinking of?! He was so dazed by the success of his fight with Snotty, he had completely forgotten Olivia. To say nothing of getting the prince back to the castle before Sir Richard and Lady Morgana arrived. What a turnip-head!

"Adolphus!" he said urgently. "We've got to get a message to the castle. We need to get Merlin or someone out here to collect the prince – but even more importantly, we need to get Olivia out of Sir Richard's chambers. You'll have to do it, you're the only one who can get there quickly enough!"

"Oh yes! Okay! Off to the castle! But, er, which bit exactly?" said Adolphus uncertainly.

Max groaned. He had felt so triumphant a minute ago and now his daring rescue seemed as if it was falling apart around him. Where should he send Adolphus, assuming Adolphus could even remember the way? And how was the young dragon going to get anyone to understand him? And what was he, Max, going to do if Sir Richard and Morgana turned up in the meantime? Should he try to get the prince away?

"Er, your highness? Do you think you can walk?"

"Oh, no, no way," said Cael cheerfully. "My legs feel like bits of string."

"Ah," said Max, heavily. Nothing for it, then. He had to face the possibility of being here when Sir Richard and that awful witch arrived. But in the meantime, Olivia needed rescuing as badly as the prince. Max remembered her small, frightened voice when he'd left, and made up his mind.

"Ferocious, you go with Adolphus. Between you, that makes one brain and one pair of wings – they should be enough to get you to Merlin's rooms. If he's not there, you'd better try to find Dad. Merlin will probably understand you, but Dad will need a note – hang on, I'll write one and tie it to Adolphus's leg."

Max found a scrap of parchment in one of Snotty's saddlebags and, using a charred stick from the fire, managed to roughly scratch out: Olivia Hogsbottom's room. Hurry!

"I hope it's still readable when you get there," he said, frowning, and rolled it up and tied it on while Adolphus did his best to stand still. "Ferocious? Are you ready?"

The black rat scampered over to Max and nipped him affectionately.

"I'll make sure we get there and I'll make sure we find Merlin, don't you worry. Much as I love your dear father, I don't think he'd last ten seconds against that le Fay woman. Just you sit tight, and if they get here before us, well, then, spit at them for me, eh, Max?"

Max laughed, shakily, and Ferocious grinned. "That's the spirit! Come on, Adolphus. We're off to the castle, quick as your wings will take us!"

He hopped on to Adolphus's back and dug in with his claws. Adolphus leaped into the air and shot off like a rocket, a streak of blue-green hurtling into the late afternoon sun, with a thin wail of "Maybe not thaat faaaaaaast!" trailing behind him.

Max smiled, and returned to the fire, where he sat hugging his knees and wondering how many seconds he could last against that le Fay woman, if he had to.

The Gagging Spell

Olivia was feeling bored, hungry and just a bit frightened. It wasn't a good combination. She seemed to have been stuck in Sir Richard's rooms for hours – certainly right through lunchtime, and probably well into the afternoon. She had tried shouting out of the window and banging on the door, but the window was too high up and there was too much noise and music down below. A couple of times someone had glanced up and seen her, but they'd obviously just thought she was waving at the crowd and they'd waved happily back. As for the door, it was heavy oak and the sound of her fists or even a chair leg on it made no more than a dull, faint thud that was not going to attract anyone's attention.

"Oh, what's happening?" she groaned for maybe the twentieth time. Why did she have to be the one stuck here on her own, with all the action happening somewhere else? Never mind having to wait until Lady Morgana got round to coming back and dealing with you, whatever that meant. Oh, why couldn't she have been the frog and Max the one who had to stay and wait? Where were they? What was happening?

Suddenly she heard footsteps in the corridor outside. She stopped stamping and stood very still, listening. Were they going to stop? Was it Sir Richard – or worse, Morgana? There was no point trying to hide as they knew she was there. All the same, she didn't like just standing there in the middle of the room. She crept into the small arched recess in the corner and pressed herself against the wall.

The footsteps stopped and there was the sound of a key in the door. Olivia held her breath as the door opened and someone came in.

"Olivia?" came an uncertain voice from across the room. Olivia gave a sigh of relief. It was Sir Richard. He might not be her favourite person in the world but he had the distinct advantage of not being Lady Morgana. She stepped out from the archway and Sir Richard jumped.

"Oh – ah! There you are... Er, I've come to let you out."

"Let me out?" said Olivia in surprise. "But I thought... Lady Morgana..."

"Ah, well, yes. She does have plans – but, well, let's just say I'm not so keen on them, myself. So I thought I'd double back here on my way out and, well, maybe forget to lock the door when I left."

Sir Richard looked pleased with himself.

A little white lie and he could stay in Lady Morgana's good books and stop any unnecessary unpleasantness occurring in his chambers.

"Fantastic!" exclaimed Olivia. "Thanks. Can I go now?"

"Oh, well, er – not so fast, young lady," said Sir Richard hurriedly. "There is the little matter of you knowing all our plans... I rather think I'm going to have to do a gagging spell on you before you scarper off to Merlin and tell all, eh?"

"A gagging spell?" said Olivia. "What's that?"

"Neat little trick I learned at Squire School," said Sir Richard proudly. "I never was much good at magic, but I rather perfected this spell over the years. Helped a lot when there was stuff I really, well, really didn't want people telling my father..." He went all misty-eyed remembering the mischief he'd got up to as a lad, but then shrugged. Never mind that – it was time to gag Olivia.

Sir Richard took a small bag from a nearby cupboard and spilled some grains of purple powder into his hand. Then he muttered a few words and flung the powder over Olivia. She felt a tingling feeling in her ears and on her tongue, but nothing else seemed to happen.

"Is that it?" she said, unimpressed.

"Indeed it is, my dear," said Sir Richard happily. "Just try to blab now and you'll find out what that little spell does."

Olivia was unconvinced, but thought it best to humour him. After all, he was going to let her go free.

"Okay," she said. "I can feel it working. Can I go now?"

"Yes, yes," said Sir Richard. "Run along, my dear. It looks like your dragon's scarpered already – out the window, eh? Probably flapping around in the castle yard. Better go and find it. I've got to go now, anyway – I've got a long ride to the forest, with my lady." And he touched the side of his nose with his finger and winked at her.

He really does believe the spell's going to

work, thought Olivia. But he was going to get a shock when she ran straight to Merlin and told him everything. She smiled blandly back at Sir Richard, sidled out of the doorway and sauntered down the corridor looking as innocent as she knew how.

***

Merlin was sitting in his large oak chair with his chin resting on his hands. He had tried everything he could think of to locate the prince, but nothing had worked. It was as if the boy had been spirited out of the castle. Yet Merlin was sure the spell wall enchantments were still working. If he stretched his mind, he could feel them still quietly wrapped around the castle walls. With a sigh he felt again for the enchantments. This time he worked his way slowly round them, testing and feeling with his thoughts, looking for the slightest waver... There! Just there! His head snapped up. He sensed the faintest, slightest tremble in the enchantment that told him it had been broken and then cunningly woven back together again to give the illusion of wholeness. Flame and thunder! What sort of wizard was he to have allowed this to happen? There was only one person who could have done it – and he was surprised even she had managed it – but clearly she had. Merlin needed to alert the king immediately. They would have to broaden the search to beyond the castle walls.

Just as he stood up, there was a timid knock at the door.

"Come in," he called, as he strapped his sword round his waist and prepared to pull his riding boots on.

A slight, dark-haired girl, wearing squire's clothes, slipped into the room. She looked familiar and Merlin frowned at her, trying to remember.

"Olivia Pendragon, sir," she said, curtsying.

"Ah, of course! I do beg your pardon. What can I do for you?"

"Well, it's about the carrot, sir," said Olivia, then stopped, and looked confused.

"Carrot?" said Merlin, gently.

"Yes!" she said, shaking her head violently. "I need to tell you, the carrot is not a parsnip." She took a deep breath and started again. "It's really important! I'm sorry, but I think a custard tart got in my ear. It's making it hard to bake cakes! Oh!!"

She almost screamed in frustration and stamped her foot on the floor. "You must help. It's urgent! The carrot is going to be steamed and the lettuce and beans have gone down to the kitchen and – oh, dungballs!!" She stopped, tears of rage and frustration in her eyes, as Merlin leaned down and took her hand.

"It's all right," he said, soothingly. "Don't try to speak. You've clearly been put under a gagging spell – I recognise the symptoms. Very frustrating, I know, it's happened to me before."

He straightened up and looked thoughtful.

"Now, the only reason I can think of for you coming to me, with a gagging spell turning everything you say into gobbledegook, is if you know something about the prince. Is that it?"

Olivia tried hard to nod, but the spell was making her shake her head. The end result was a kind of dizzy corkscrew movement that almost made her fall over.

"I'll take that as a yes," said Merlin grimly. "Now, what are we going to do? I can take the spell off, but it's a tricky one – sometimes takes hours... If they haven't completely gagged you, it may be that you can write?"

Olivia nodded. Brilliant. Why hadn't she thought of that? Eagerly she took the parchment Merlin gave her and started to scribble as fast as she could. After a few sentences, she glanced back over what she'd written and nearly cried.

The cook needs to put more salt in the stew because the parsnips taste like old boots and the carrots are as mouldy as a pair of old...

"Oh!!" shouted Olivia, and threw the quill she was holding at the wall. Just as its ink spattered onto the floor, there was a tremendous crash and a small dragon hurtled in through the door, hit the wall and tumbled to the floor in front of them. Immediately he scrabbled to his feet with a wild flapping of wings.

"Sir, sir!" panted Adolphus, and held out his claw with a crumpled piece of parchment tied to it. "Quick! You have to rescue Olivia! And Max! And the prince! Quickly!"

"Adolphus!" shrieked Olivia, as she threw her arms round him, dislodging the large black rat clinging to his back.

"Oh, that's all right," said Ferocious, grumpily picking himself back up. "Don't mind me. I'll be fine. Just about had my whiskers blown out by the wind as we flew here and all my fur's sticking out the wrong way, but never mind. Knock me flying why don't you, just to finish off the journey nicely."

"Ferocious, don't be such a grump," said Olivia, fondly, stroking his fur down the right way. She turned to Merlin, who had taken the parchment and was reading it.

"This is Adolphus," explained Olivia, glad that the spell didn't seem to affect what she said, so long as it was not about the prince. "My dragon. And Ferocious – Max's rat. They were with Max when he went..." She stopped. "Oh, what's the point? I'll just end up telling you they went to the dung heap to pick some bluebells!"

"The note says that you need rescuing from 'Hogsbottom's Room'. Is that where you were?" Olivia nodded. Merlin looked thoughtful. "And the dragon has just come from Max and the prince?"

"Yes," she said.

"Then I think we had better get there as soon as we can. Ferocious can give me the details as we ride."

"You can understand them?" said Olivia, surprised.

Merlin smiled. "Having once been an animal has that effect, as you have found – and Max is not the only young wizard to have discovered a spell to do that. But we need to hurry, it sounds as if a rescue operation is needed. And I think we should all go together – for the moment, you will be safer with me than in the castle."

"Yes, yes!" said Adolphus, flapping around the room. "We need to go! Quickly! Or they'll get to Max before we do! Quick! Quick! Quick!"

A True Knight

It was starting to get a little chilly in the small hut in the forest. The late afternoon sun hardly penetrated the thick forest canopy and the fire Adolphus had started was dying down. There was no more wood in the hut and Max didn't really want to leave the prince and look for more outside. He shivered.

"How long do you think they've been gone?"

he asked the prince.

"It feels like ages," said Cael, throwing himself backwards on the bed and trying to wriggle his legs. "I wish I could walk! At least we could go and hide somewhere!"

"I'm not sure it would do any good," said Max gloomily. "Lady Morgana's a witch, she'd find us instantly."

"Well you're a wizard, aren't you? Can't you make us invisible? Or something even better? Can't you turn us into dragons?"

"I'm not really a wizard," said Max, with a sigh. "I'm just learning."

There was a muffled noise from the corner, where Snotty was wriggling violently on the floor and trying to speak. He had come to a few minutes before, but so far Max had ignored him, apart from checking that the gag and ropes binding him were secure. Max glanced in his direction and wondered whether to throw a sack over his head. Snotty tried hard to say something. It sounded suspiciously like,

"Undo me, you pea-brained pile of dragon's dung."

Max raised his eyebrows at Snotty.

"Temper, temper!" he said while Snotty writhed angrily and kicked the side of the hut. "Keep quiet or I'll turn you into a frog."

Snotty looked sceptical.

"I can, you know," said Max. "You wait till the competition tomorrow, then you'll see!"

Except there probably won't be a competition tomorrow, thought Max gloomily. Or if there was, he wouldn't be there, because he'd have been chopped into small pieces by Morgana and fed to the forest wolves... What a waste of all that frogspell potion he'd brewed up.

Wait a minute! Frogspell potion! It was in his pouch! It had been there all along, ever since Merlin's rooms when he'd given a drop to Olivia and put the bottle in his pouch. What a dung-brain not to have thought of it before! Quickly he felt around for it, and then drew the small blue glass bottle out in triumph. It was unharmed – and still three-quarters full.

"Ha! Eat dirt, Snotty! Because this will turn you into a frog quicker than you can say 'Max is a genius' if you so much as think about whispering any more insults!"

Snotty made a face, but Max noticed that he stopped wriggling and didn't try to say anything either. Max grinned. That had shut Snotty up, anyway. But better than that – he now had something he could use if Sir Richard and Lady Morgana turned up. The question was, should he use the potion to turn himself and the prince into frogs, so they could hide – or should he use the spell against them?

Max sat down slowly by what was left of the fire, holding the blue bottle of frogspell potion and thinking hard. If he turned himself and Cael into frogs, they had a good chance of escaping, and Merlin would be able to change them back with a wave of his hand when he arrived. If he arrived. But then there was the chance they would get caught by Morgana anyway – and Max really didn't fancy being a frog if that happened.

The alternative was to try to turn Sir Richard and Lady Morgana into frogs when they arrived – but Max was just an eleven-year-old apprentice wizard with one small potion bottle and Lady Morgana was the most powerful enchantress in the land. For all Max knew, the spell wouldn't even work on her, or she might whip it out of the air by magic and send it hurtling back towards him. Max shuddered, remembering her pale eyes, honey voice and icy, tinkling laughter. But then he thought about the last time he had gone to his father and asked not to be a knight because he was rubbish at swordplay.

"Being a knight isn't about how good you are with a sword, Max," Sir Bertram had said, holding him by the shoulders and looking at him seriously. "Being a knight is about facing up to your fears, sticking up for others even if you're scared, doing your best even when you think you're no good. Even wizards need to be a knight first and foremost. And I know you can be a good knight, Max. I know you've got it in you." Then he had slapped Max on the back so hard he nearly sent him flying and told him to "get out there and give them hell." So Max, inspired, had climbed back on his horse and whacked at the practice dummy so hard that he would have sliced its head off with one blow if his horse hadn't shied at the last minute so that he fell off instead.

Remembering this conversation now, Max smiled. He knew what Sir Bertram would have said to his dilemma. Max sighed, and went to find a good place to hide near the door of the hut.

***

"I don't know what can have happened to Adrian, my lady," apologised Sir Richard, sweating inside his heavy riding cloak. Drat the boy! Where was he? Why weren't the horses here? Had they made it through the forest?

"It does seem rather – inefficient – Sir Richard," said Lady Morgana in her low, sweet voice. "But no matter. I'm sure they'll be here in good time. Perhaps we should wait in the hut?"

"Of course, my lady, splendid idea. If you'll

128

just permit me to take your hand?" Take her hand! thought Sir Richard, over the moon. Him! Holding the arm of the most powerful woman in the whole kingdom! He was really on the way up! He chortled happily to himself as they crossed the threshold together.

His eyes had barely taken in the sight of Snotty, lying tied up and gagged on the stone floor of the hut, when he was hit in the face by a blob of blue gunk. The next thing he knew, the room had gone all shivery and strange, and he was suddenly very much shorter than usual. Next to him was what seemed like an unnaturally large, acid-green frog with violently puce spots, looking as angry as he had ever seen a frog look. A second later, there was a pop! and the frog disappeared.

"Phew!" said Max, sitting down suddenly on the stone floor of the hut. "I'm glad that's over."

The single remaining frog, a sludgy brown one with orange spots, croaked at him reprovingly.

"Max Pendragon," it said in a deep frog voice.

"I am very disappointed in you. Turning respectable grown-ups into frogs! I think I might have to have words with your father. Turn me back this instant!"

"Not likely," muttered Max. He scooped the frog up and put it in his belt pouch, where he couldn't hear it croaking any more, and then turned to the prince.

"Well, your highness. It looks like we're safe now. We just have to wait for Merlin to arrive."

"That was brilliant," said Cael, wide-eyed.

Max grinned. "Yes, it was pretty cool, wasn't it?" he said happily.

***

When Merlin and the others arrived at the hut in the forest, Max had collected enough wood to get the fire roaring and brewed up a whole cauldron of spiced apple juice. He and Cael were sitting happily by the fire munching the rest of Snotty's supplies and telling bad jokes.

"Well, well," said Merlin as he crossed the threshold. "It appears we are rather too late for doing any rescuing. You seem to have rescued yourselves pretty thoroughly."

"Max was amazing!" said Cael, jumping up and staggering over to hug Merlin. His legs were still not quite right, but the spell was wearing off fast. "He punched the big boy and then turned the grown-ups into frogs! He's a really good wizard, Merlin. Even better than you!"

Max swallowed and went pink. But he didn't have time to protest because Olivia hurled herself at him and gave him a huge bear hug and Ferocious scampered over and nipped his ankles affectionately. Meanwhile, Adolphus flapped around their heads getting his feet and wings tangled up in his excitement.

"You're okay, Max, you're okay! I'm so glad! We had no idea what had happened!" exclaimed Olivia when she had enough breath. "I can't believe you sorted out Sir Richard and her! You must have been terrified!"

"Oh it was nothing," said Max airily, but

then he caught Merlin's piercing grey eyes and decided he had better be truthful. "Actually, I was terrified," he admitted.

"And so you should have been," said Merlin. "Morgana le Fay is an extremely dangerous and powerful sorceress. You did very well to deal with her as successfully as you obviously have. I presume she – ah – disappeared after you changed her?"

"Yes, there was a sort of pop and she was gone. But I've got Sir Richard in my belt pouch."

Merlin laughed, a rich, warm and infectious laugh that they all found themselves joining in with, and then clapped Max on the shoulder.

"Well done, Max, really! A most extraordinary spell, and you showed real bravery to see it through. It takes a special sort of magic to brew up a frogspell potion, most rare and unusual – I am glad to see the ability goes with a good heart and courage as well. You'll make a fine wizard, my boy, very fine indeed!"

Max felt warm all over at the praise, but

looking up at this fierce, tall knight, so unlike the Merlin he'd imagined, he knew that he had to be honest.

"Actually," he said. "I didn't exactly make the frogspell, it was more of an accident... And I only knocked Snotty over by accident too. And I had my eyes closed when I threw the potion at Lady Morgana. If I'd had them open I'd probably have missed."

Merlin looked down at Max gravely, and then smiled. "Max – you are very honest. But it's not just the ingredients that make a frogspell. It may have been an accident to start with, but only a very powerful sort of magic will make it work. And if you did knock this young squire over by accident, or hit my lady by accident, you did so because you were standing up to them in the first place – which takes a good deal of courage. I think you have a most unusual sort of magic, and a good heart, Max Pendragon, and I shall watch your next 'accident' with interest."

Max looked up at Merlin's bright eyes and hawklike face and suddenly felt six feet tall. He knew he would follow Merlin to the end of the world if he could. He grinned, and Merlin clapped him on the shoulder again.

"Still," he sighed. "There is little doubt that my lady is long gone, and will certainly have a very good alibi prepared for her part in this. And unfortunately, she is likely to get away with it. The king has a very forgiving heart where that lady is concerned. Too forgiving, I fear," he added, looking grim.

Then he smiled at them all and said, "Right! Enough standing around. I think it's time we headed back to the castle. We need to take this princeling back to his mother, and while we're at it, we'd better take this well-trussed up young man and his befrogged father to the king!"

The Spell-Making Competition

Sir Bertram Pendragon was happier than he had been in a long time. Happier even than he'd been when he pushed his worst enemy, Sir Richard Hogsbottom, in the castle duck pond after a particularly heated game of 'Who Can Spit Furthest'. He couldn't get enough of the story of how Max and Olivia had between them foiled the plot to kidnap the Cornish prince, especially the bit where Max felled Sir Richard's ghastly son Adrian with a knockout punch. The story had been carefully edited, to leave out all mention of magic, frogs, Lady Morgana or the fact that it had taken place so far away. Sir Bertram was rather under the impression that Max and Olivia had come across Snotty guarding the prince in an old cellar somewhere, and that was the way King Arthur wanted it left.

"I am most grateful to Max and Olivia," he'd said gravely, when Sir Bertram had arrived to collect his children late in the afternoon before. "They have helped us avoid a major embarrassment. But I'm afraid their exploits must stay a secret. There are too many enemies who would like to make something of this. If it were known I had almost failed to keep Cael safe..." He sighed, and his blue eyes clouded over for a second, then he shrugged. "But let's try not to think of that. The prince is now happily with his mother and none the worse for his adventure. Merlin has made sure that all he remembers is wandering off to play with Max and Olivia. As for Sir Richard..." Arthur grimaced. "He has been sent to a post in the northern marches of the kingdom, out of trouble. He, his son and his ward, Jerome, are leaving this afternoon. And there's no trace of the unknown witch they say was behind it all."

"Well, she's not that far away—" began Olivia, but Arthur stopped her with a look and put his fingers on his lips. He looked so careworn and sad that Olivia wanted to give him a hug, but didn't quite dare.

"Cael's been found, and that's what matters," said Arthur. "We must just put it behind us, and be more careful in future." Then he turned to Max and Olivia, and smiled warmly. "My heartfelt thanks to my two newest members of court," he said, and they each felt a burst of pride and happiness travel from their head to their toes as he looked at them. Max felt he could understand why King Arthur's knights all adored him so much. But he could see Merlin looking grim, nearby, and remembered his words about the king being too forgiving. Arthur had accepted Morgana's well-prepared alibi, firmly backed up by Sir Richard and Snotty. He had decided that Max and Olivia must have been mistaken, and it had been some other mysterious witch behind the plot, who had apparently bespelled Sir Richard and his son into helping her. So Lady Morgana was still at court. Max wondered how much more trouble would come from the king's stubborn belief in those he loved...

Sir Bertram, however, was as happy as a dragon with a mountain of gold.

"Max, my boy! I'm so proud of you!" he burst out at regular intervals, clapping his son on the shoulder heartily. "I knew you had it in you! Straight upper cut to the chin, was it, eh?"

"Er, not exactly," said Max, who had tried to explain that it was more of a knockout push than a knockout punch, but Sir Bertram didn't really care.

"Takes a lot of guts to stand up to a bigger boy," he'd said, solemnly. "I'm glad to know that you will stand up for what's right, and I'm prouder of you and Olivia than you can possibly know. And besides," he'd added, rubbing his hands with glee, "It's certainly one in the eye for old Hogsbottom, eh? Ha! He looked like a scarecrow with all the straw taken out of him when he left yesterday. 'How's Adrian?' I said. He looked like he wanted to kill me! Ha, ha! And now he's going to be stuck up in the northern marches, guarding a swamp. Nothing there but mud and slime and marshes! Serves him right!"

Max had been enjoying the praise and attention all morning. Even more so when he started noticing Olivia pretending to be sick every time Sir Bertram mentioned the knockout punch again – which he did about every five minutes. But his enjoyment was gradually being replaced by nerves as the time for the Novices' Spell-Making Competition approached.

Despite all the nice things Merlin had said about his rare and unusual magic, if Max couldn't persuade his father that he should train as a wizard, he wouldn't get much of a chance to do anything with it. Punching Snotty Hogsbottom had unfortunately made Sir Bertram even more convinced Max would make a fine knight after all. It had made it even more important for Max to show what a great wizard he could be. He needed something big and impressive. He needed to show Sir Bertram that magic was as good as punches. He still needed to win the Novices' Spell-making Competition.

***

In all the bustle of the morning, Max and Olivia had had no time to get together and practise their act for the competition. It was almost time and Max was hurriedly preparing his robes and spell bottles.

"Olivia?" he called across from the corner of their chambers where he was half buried under a pile of cloaks and saddlebags. "Where's the antidote bottle?"

"How should I know?" said Olivia. "You had it last. It's probably in your pouch."

"No it isn't," said Max in frustration. "I've got the frogspell bottle, but the other one's disappeared..."

"That'll be good then," said Ferocious. "Turn her into a frog, can't turn her back. Marvellous. Should definitely win with that one."

"Actually," said Max, turning to Ferocious. "I can turn her back. Or rather, you can. I think I must have left the antidote in the forest, but I've just had a fabulous idea. I could just make some smoke on stage and then you could use it as cover to sneak out and kiss her back!"

"No way!" shouted Olivia and "Absolutely not!" shouted Ferocious at exactly the same time and with pretty much the same tone of disgust. But after a massive amount of persuasion on Max's part they eventually agreed. Olivia finally said that being kissed by Ferocious couldn't possibly be worse than being kissed by Max, and Ferocious decided that he was just about prepared to do it for the right to eat all of Max's bacon rind for the next year.

***

The castle green was cleared of stalls and a large stage had been put up in the middle, decked with banners and streamers. Most of the assorted knights, ladies, wizards and witches at the festival were seated in front of the stage, watching a small boy bewitching an arrow to fly around in circles and clapping politely. Lady Griselda and Sir Bertram were sitting near the front. She was trying to look encouraging and he was trying not to look bored. Max and Olivia were waiting nervously by the stage for their turn to be called. Ferocious poked his head out of Max's pocket and surveyed the scene.

"It won't work, you know," he said gloomily. "Something's bound to go wrong. Turn your sister into a badger most likely, and then we won't be able to turn her back. Goodness knows what works with badgers."

"Shut up Ferocious!" whispered Olivia. "Just do your bit and it will be fine."

Adolphus bounded up beside them.

"Hello! Hello! All set? It's really exciting! What fun!"

Max didn't reply. He was actually feeling rather ill. What if it didn't work? What if the potion had gone off since yesterday? What if Olivia did get stuck as a frog? Or worse, what if she just stayed a girl and the other novices laughed their heads off at Max's feeble spell? They were all extremely surprised about Snotty Hogsbottom's sudden disappearance for the wild northern marches. It had left the competition wide open and everyone now felt they might be in with a chance of winning. But no one was expecting the winner to be the person who always came last, Max 'extremely accident-prone' Pendragon. He swallowed. No going back now. It was nearly his turn. Just Owain Tregarth to go, one of Snotty's particular cronies.

The boy on stage, who had successfully turned a blue jug into a purple one with white spots, left to mild applause and the presiding wizard called out, "Owain Tregarth, of Castle Blackroot!"

Owain gave Max and Olivia a black look as he pushed past them and stepped onto the stage. He took a potion bottle out of one pocket and an egg out of the other, sprinkled some of the potion on the egg and stepped back smartly.

There was a WHOOMPH and a cloud of silvery smoke. When it cleared, the egg had grown to the size of a person. It cracked, and out stepped an enormous peacock with a magnificent blue-green tail. The peacock shrieked and strutted about the stage for a minute, then gradually started to shrink. When the bird reached the size of a mouse, Owain stepped forward and captured it in the remains of eggshell, which at once became a normal-sized, whole egg once more. There was a burst of applause and Owain looked around at the audience and smirked. He was pretty sure he had just won the Novices' Cup.

"Wow!" said Adolphus, as the audience cheered and clapped. "That was brilliant!"

"Whose side are you on?" said Max fiercely.

"That was nothing special! It's only a growth and reversal spell combined. Just because he happened to have a fancy peacock's egg doesn't make it anything new! I've done one of those before, anyway!"

"That would be the time you made that egg – er – well – a slightly bigger egg, then, would it?" said Ferocious innocently.

Olivia stamped her foot.

"Stop it, you two! Max's right! The point is, no novice has ever turned someone into a frog before! That's got to be a winning spell."

But even she was worried. Owain's spell had definitely been impressive. They really needed the frogspell to be perfect.

A Winning Spell

"And now," announced the presiding wizard, "Max Pendragon, of Castle Perilous!"

The audience clapped politely. Sir Bertram cheered loudly, but Lady Griselda was hiding her face in her hands and peeping through her fingers. Adolphus, meanwhile, was bounding about like a bouncy ball breathing fire into the air.

"I shall be turning my sister into a frog, and

then back into a girl," announced Max, looking very nervous. He could see his parents just below him and Merlin leaning casually against a tree and watching from the back. Merlin winked. Max turned to Olivia and took the blue glass potion bottle from his pouch. Wearing gloves, he carefully shook a small piece of sticky blue goo out of the bottle and chucked it at Olivia.

Bang!

She disappeared – and in her place was a purple and red frog. The audience gasped, then stamped and cheered. Sir Bertram turned to his astonished wife and grinned widely.

"Well, that's something, eh? Never knew he could do something like that! Knockout punch and the best spell in the competition by far! Well, well."

Max sighed with relief. It had worked! Now for the tricky bit. He scattered some smoke powder on the stage and wreaths of purple smoke surrounded Olivia.

"Now!" he hissed at Ferocious, and

Ferocious jumped.

When the smoke cleared, there were two black rats sitting in the middle of the stage, looking extremely surprised.

The audience gasped. People turned to each other and started to mutter. Lady Griselda whimpered, and Sir Bertram looked distinctly worried, but Merlin was looking amused and he gave Max a friendly grin. Max gulped.

"Behold!" he cried, recovering from his horror. "From one frog, to two rats! And now..." He scattered smoke powder again and dived into the middle of it. When the smoke cleared this time, he had one arm firmly round his sister, and a bulge in his belt pouch.

"... Back to a person again!" he shouted triumphantly, wiping the sweat from his brow. The audience clapped and cheered and whooped, and Max could see Lady Griselda hugging Sir Bertram in relief.

"What happened?" said Olivia when they

were safely back off stage. "Why didn't it work?"

"I suppose it must only work properly with a human kiss," said Max thoughtfully. "Any other animal just turns you into one of them."

"Well, it proves Mrs Mudfoot must be human, I suppose," said Olivia. "I always wondered. Anyway – it was brilliant, Max, really – you're bound to win, the audience loved it!"

They were distracted by a deep booming voice, which suddenly rang out across the castle green.

"And now," said the voice, "The prize presentation for the Novices' Spell-Making Cup..."

Max and Olivia pushed nearer to the front and Max crossed his fingers and hoped with all his strength.

"Step forward, our judge: the distinguished enchantress, and sister to the king – Lady Morgana le Fay!"

Max and Olivia looked at each other in horror.

"I didn't know she was judging!" hissed Max.

"No, neither did I... We're sunk, Max – she'll

never give you the prize!"

Lady Morgana, looking serene and glamorous, her long black hair framing her smooth, pale face, glided to the centre of the stage and looked around at her audience.

"Yes, well, an extraordinary display of talent," she said in her honey voice. "Wonderful spells from all who entered – really wonderful." She smiled at them all, apparently sincerely, but when her eye passed over Max he felt a shiver down his spine and his toes curled.

"Sadly there can be only one winner. I was very impressed by the growth and reversal spell of the marvellous novice from Castle Blackroot..."

"Here it comes," whispered Max gloomily to Olivia as the audience cheered. But he was wrong.

"However, I think we all know, even without a deep understanding of magic, that turning a person into a frog is something quite marvellously rare – something that has certainly never been seen in a Novices' Competition before – and I therefore award the Novices' Spell-Making Cup to – Max Pendragon!"

Max was stunned. He looked up at Lady Morgana and she smiled at him, and this time her blue eyes were full of apparent warmth and admiration. He could even see the resemblance to King Arthur in her face as she held out the gold cup that was his prize. Max was completely taken aback by this change and only managed to mutter a few garbled words as the audience cheered and Sir Bertram stamped his feet. He looked across at Olivia who appeared almost as stunned as he was, but her eyes were narrowed as she watched Morgana. His sister clearly didn't trust her an inch.

Lady Morgana took Max's hand and raised it up, and then she gestured to the audience for quiet.

"This year, as the judge, I have a special extra prize to award," she announced sweetly. "Max Pendragon, the worthy winner, shall have a free place at my Summer Spell School at Castle Gore. He may stay as my guest for the whole six weeks and I shall especially enjoy teaching such a talented young man some of my most interesting potions." She looked around and smiled as the audience clapped and cheered happily. Only Merlin, at the back, looked thoughtful.

Max was clutching his cup and still feeling slightly stunned when he saw Sir Bertram and Lady Griselda approaching across the grass. They were smiling and Lady Griselda gave Max a hug.

"Max, darling," she said. "You did brilliantly

to win the competition! It seems you're destined to be a wizard rather than a knight, after all."

Max looked questioningly at his father and saw him nodding vigorously.

"Too right!" said Sir Bertram. "Damned marvellous spell, that, marvellous! Had everyone completely on the edge of their seats! Frog – rat – Olivia! Really gave me a bit of a turn there, in the middle. Thought I'd end up with a rat for a daughter, eh, Olivia?!" He laughed heartily, while Max tried to look like he had meant it that way all along. "Point is, Max, Lady Morgana le Fay is a very powerful enchantress and she knows a good spell when she sees one. So even though you do pack a great punch," he looked wistful for a moment, "it looks like it's a wizard apprenticeship for you, my boy!"

Olivia whooped and gave Max a big hug. "You did it, Max – you're going to be a wizard! Now I can be a knight!"

"Ah, well, just a minute, just a minute," said

Sir Bertram quickly. "First of all, girls can't be knights. And second of all, there's something Max has to do before it's completely decided."

Max felt his heart sink. He had a terrible feeling he knew what the something was going to be.

"We want to be absolutely sure it's the right thing, Max," said Lady Griselda. "That means a bit more than just one good spell. Lady Morgana's offer is a fantastic opportunity – her Summer Spell School is renowned across the kingdom. If you come back from it with a Merit Certificate, we'll find someone to take you on as a full apprentice."

"But you'll still have to learn to wield a sword," added Sir Bertram, clapping him on the back. "You never know when it might be useful."

Max exchanged glances with Olivia and grimaced. Skill with a sword might come in useful quite soon, he thought, as he contemplated six weeks at Castle Gore with a dangerous sorceress who probably wanted him dead.

***

Max and Olivia threw themselves down on the grass by the moat and stretched out in the late afternoon sunshine. The birds were singing fit to burst, the trout in the moat were lazily snapping at the flies hovering over the surface, and they could smell the festival feast being prepared in the castle yard. It was a glorious day, and Max had just won the Novices' Cup and a half share of twenty gold coins. He should have been over the moon. But there was the little matter of spending the summer in the company of Lady Morgana, trying his best to stay alive.

"Do you think she's really that bad?" he said to Olivia, as he chewed thoughtfully on a piece of grass. "She almost seemed nice when she invited me to the Spell School. And the king trusts her."

Olivia snorted. "You must be joking. She's just good at putting on an act. She's about as likely to stop being evil as a pike is to stop eating small frogs."

Max sighed. He thought so too. In fact, every time he thought about the Spell School, a cold trickle of anxiety ran down the back of his neck.

"No, it's no good thinking she'll change," said Olivia decisively. "She's up to something, Max, face it. What you need is a few trusty companions with you in Gore. We just have to figure out a way to get me, Adolphus and Ferocious along too."

Max sat up.

"Really? Would you really all come?"

"Well of course I'm coming," said Ferocious crossly. "Can't believe you thought I wouldn't be there. You know me – always willing to lose a whisker in a good cause. Ready to brave the wickedest enchantress in the world. If she tries anything, I'll bite her toes off..."

Max considered this. It would be easy to hide Ferocious in his tunic or saddlebags. But Olivia and Adolphus?

"It won't work," he sighed, thinking about it.

"Dad will never let you come."

"Dad," said Olivia with a very determined expression, "will not be able to do anything about it. I'm coming, Max, whether you like it or not. So get used to it!"

Max looked at his younger sister and thought that, however unlikely it seemed, she might just manage it. He grinned, and suddenly felt a whole lot better.

"And remember," added Olivia, "we still have the frogspell potion. We can turn ourselves into frogs whenever we want. Hey – we can be rats too, and dragons if we don't mind being kissed by Adolphus!... I really fancy being a dragon!"

"Oh yes!" said Adolphus happily. "Yes, please! Can I be a dragon too? How exciting!"

"You are a dragon, pea-brain," Ferocious pointed out. "Better not put Adolphus in charge of anything important in these plans, or we'll all end up in the duck pond."

Max grinned, and stretched out in the

sunshine, thinking that he'd probably got a fun summer ahead of him after all. He'd manage Gore somehow, and then, when he came back, he'd get proper wizard lessons at last. He wouldn't ever have to learn to joust! How good was that? And Snotty Hogsbottom had been banished to the outer reaches of the marshy northern borders and was probably covered in mud and slime at that very moment. And all because he had accidentally discovered the frogspell. Really, what could be better?

Coming soon...

CAULDRON SPELLS

Max Pendragon is really not looking forward to
attending Morgana Le Fay's summer Spell School.
Not only is his battered cauldron producing slimy
green sludge instead of perfect spells, but ever since
he and his sister Olivia foiled evil Morgana's plot
against King Arthur, they have been wary of her
plans for revenge.

Max and Olivia soon discover that Spell School
has more in store for them than they could ever
imagine, and it's not long before the siblings find
themselves entangled in Morgana's nasty schemes.
With the help of Merlin and a mysterious bard,
Caradoc, will they be able to outwit Morgana and
save Arthur for a second time?

Join Max and Olivia for more magical thrills,
spills and spells in 2012!